PETUNIA'S PANDEMONIUM

SEA SHENANIGANS, BOOK 5

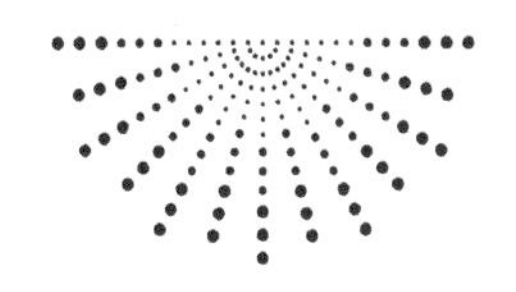

ROBYN PETERMAN

JOIN MY NEWSLETTER!

This book is a work of fiction. Names, characters, places, and incidents either are the product of the author's imagination or are used fictitiously. Any resemblance to actual persons, living or dead, businesses, companies, events, or locales is coincidental.

This book contains content that may not be suitable for young readers 17 and under.

❀ Created with Vellum

ACKNOWLEDGMENTS

The Sea Shenanigans characters have been inside my head for quite a while and I adore each and every one of them! Letting amy inner mermaid out has been fun. I can't wait for you guys to read this book. Petunia's Pandemonium was a blast to write. Petunia and Delphinus are every kind of crazy and hilarious.

As always, I write the book, but it takes a whole lot of wonderful people to make the magic happen. I am a lucky girl because I have a whole lot of wonderful people in my life.

Wanda, you are magical. Thank you.

Donna McDonald, thank you. You are the most brilliant MYST partner in the world!

My beta readers—Wanda and Susan thank you. I adore you.

Renee George, you are the best hand-holder and Cookie a gal could have. I love you.

And to my readers… thank you. I do this for you.

Steve, Henry and Audrey, thank you. I love you and you make everything worth it.

DEDICATION

For my own magic Genie named Steve.
You are all my wishes come true.

BOOK DESCRIPTION

Mix one part Mermaid—one part Genie. Throw in an intoxicated God of the Sea and and a few smack-talking Pirates. What have you got?

Pandemonium.

Petunia's Pandemonium to be more accurate.

Petunia

Letting the ocean current take me where it may for the last twenty-five years hasn't worked out so great. So, instead of getting my tail in a knot, I'm making some swimmingly simple changes.

—Stay on Mystical Isle with my cousins who love me.

—Avenge my parents and eliminate the sea monster who's wreaking havoc.

—Forget about the gorgeous, no-good Genie who left me at the altar... so to speak.

—Stay away from Genies until the end of time.

—Join Poseidon's embarrassingly named online dating service for Immortals and get back into the game.

What could go wrong?

Del

I'm a Genie in a bottle baby. Or at least I was. After spending a quarter of a century, doing time for streaking at the Super Bowl after being destroyed by love, I'm a free man. It's time to get my life together and forget about the Mermaid who didn't want me. The list is simple.

—Stop granting wishes to idiots.

—Figure out why the Genie Star Fire Light in my eyes is burning out before I die a slow agonizing death.

—Eat an outstanding cheeseburger.

—Stay away from Mermaids.

—Join Poseidon's embarrassingly named online dating service for Immortals and get back into the game.

It's a plan. Not necessarily a stellar one, but it's a plan.

Come for the Vacation. Stay for the Shenanigans!

1

PETUNIA

"Ahoy, Petunia! If ye might be needin' a BFF, I'd be delighted to be at yer service," the strange-looking little man said, peeping into the open door of my beach hut.

His hat bore a skull-and-crossbones. In what I assumed was an attempt at good manners, he removed his head-wear and held it smashed against his scrawny chest. My visitor's hair was sparse and his nose was crooked as if he'd brawled repeatedly and lost most of the time. However, his eyes twinkled and his smile was sweet in an alarming, gap-toothed way. My potential BFF sported royal-blue breeches that had seen better days, knee-high boots and a shirt with so much ruffled material it could have passed for a dress.

Sighing dramatically, I closed my eyes and shook my head. This was a new ploy and it wasn't going to work better than any of the others. My cousins were determined for me to be happy and were clearly resorting to desperate measures at this point. I certainly didn't need an ancient

Pirate as a BFF. Honestly, a couple of hours of retail therapy followed by a massage and a pedicure would be far better than getting attached to a tiny balding Pirate with questionable fashion sense. People never stayed around. So, neither did I.

I'd been holed up in my hut 24-7 for a few weeks. Well, not exactly. I swam in the ocean at night under the stars while everyone slept. Less complicated that way.

"Not interested in a BFF," I lied as I gave him a look that would have sent most running for their lives.

This one didn't run. He was either daft or had a death wish.

The little Pirate ignored the warning glare and ambled right into my swanky temporary abode. Making himself comfortable on the shimmering seashell encrusted chaise lounge, he removed his boots and wiggled his skinny, hairy toes.

"I didn't take ye for a green-gilled, cowardly tar stain," he commented casually, raising a bushy brow at me.

For a brief moment I felt like a teenager being reprimanded by my father, if my father had been a scrawny Pirate—which he wasn't. He was a Merman—strong and wise… and gone.

The feeling was fleeting, but it brought back long-forgotten memories of feeling safe and loved. I quickly pushed the ludicrous thought aside. I was a two-hundred-year-old Mermaid. My parents had been gone for a century thanks to a vicious sea monster. I was on my own and I was going to stay that way.

Narrowing my eyes at my unwanted guest, I tamped

back my instinct to drop-kick the little dude right back out the way he came in. "What language are you speaking?"

"Pirate," he replied with a grin and what I could only describe as a giggle.

I almost smiled.

Almost.

"Name?" I inquired, pressing my lips together so I didn't reveal my amusement. He'd never leave if he'd thought he'd won. He seemed like a determined little bastard.

Puffing his bony chest out then bowing gallantly, my new buddy slowly slid into a right split and raised his arms in the air.

"Upton 'Iron Chest' Driscol," he announced and then adjusted his position so he could display his left split. "Me friends just call me Upton or arsehole."

I was shocked to silence… and impressed. The day had gone from simply boring and depressing to *bizarre*, boring and depressing. How could an elderly Pirate who answered to arsehole do the splits and I couldn't? Well, at least I'd found a new life goal. While being immortal was awesome most of the time, it could get monotonous. You had to have aspirations for growth—or at the very least, the splits—or you would go crazy.

"You're very limber," I pointed out while considering giving the splits a try. I was immortal and healed quickly. If I ripped a hamstring, I'd be fine within the hour.

"Aye," Upton said with pride. "I can lick me own nards."

Again… speechless.

I was hoping I'd heard him wrong, but then he demonstrated. Thankfully, he was clothed.

"Umm… Upton," I choked out on a gag.

"Aye, swimmin' hooker?" he inquired politely, glancing up from his lewd contortionist act.

"If you insist on doing that, I'm going to call you Upchuck. I would think that might be enough to curb your unappetizing habit. However, I'm gonna go out on a limb and guess that name calling won't do the trick since you also answer to arsehole. So, if being referred to as Upchuck isn't gonna do it and you continue to become one with your privates, I'll zap your nards clean off your body. Also, if you call me a swimming hooker ever again, I'll pick you up and throw your ass so far out into the ocean it will take you a month to swim back. You feel me?"

"Yar a violent eyeliner wearin' dinghy dangler of a wench," Upton said with a nod of approval and a thumbs up.

Again, I had to hold back my amusement. The little idiot was kind of charming in an uncouth way.

"Thank you," I replied. A compliment was a compliment no matter how gross. "We clear about you leaving your man berries out of your mouth? It would be a real shame if I had to perform a ballsectomy."

"So yar is sayin' I shouldn't cleanse me bits?" Upton asked trying to work out the particulars of my threat.

Slowly blowing my breath out between partially clenched lips, I did my best not to laugh. Watching Upton have a go at his package wasn't remotely funny… or maybe it was. I needed help.

"How about this," I offered, not wanting to be mean to someone who was extending friendship—no matter how odd he was. "Why don't you stick to slurping on your junk in the privacy of your own home—as long as there are no people within three thousand yards or so."

Upton considered my suggestion and then nodded his head thoughtfully. "Blimey, I suppose I could scour me danglers on the poop deck or possibly in the head. Ye make a fine point, Mermaid Petunia. Swabbin' me nickel ticklers in public might be why I'm havin' a hard time keepin' mateys. Although, methinks the weevil eatin', rum swiggin' sea serpents are green at the gills at me talent for disinfecting me chumblies."

"Mmmkay, I understood very little of that," I said, squinting at Upton in confusion. "And that's probably a good thing. Just keep your lips off your jibblies and we're good."

Upton smiled wide and a little giggle left his lips. "So, ye *do* want me to be yer BFF?"

Sighing, I was tempted to say yes. I was lonely—which was entirely my own fault. My cousins, Tallulah, Ariel, Misty and Madison had done everything they could think of to make me happy and feel welcome on their island. It was so lovely it made me itch.

Good never lasted long in my life. I was bad luck. Getting used to being cared for and loved was dangerous. It always ended. Always.

"Not in the market for a BFF," I told Upton as I stood and indicated he should exit my hut. "I'm leaving the Mystical Isle soon."

Upton's chin dropped to his chest. He stared at his hands and sniffled.

Shit on a seashell. Had I made him cry?

"Is it because I tongue sponged me gangoolies?" he asked as fat salty tears ran down his cheeks. "Me mateys call me a greasy-haired sea rat. Mebbe the peg-legged bow bunglers are right. Ye would be ashamed to have a BFF like me."

"Of course, they're *not* right," I sputtered before I thought about the consequences of making Upton feel better. "You don't have enough hair for it to be greasy. And you are not a rat. I mean, you're kind of tiny, but rats can't do the splits. I suppose they might be able to lick their marbles—but that's not the point here and it's disgusting. Plus, I think puking in my mouth right now would be counterproductive. Most importantly, I would not be ashamed to have you for a BFF. Any Mermaid would be lucky to have such a limber best friend forever."

Slapping my hand over my mouth, I realized I'd gone too far. The mini-Pirate shrieked with joy and was so delighted he did a barefoot jig around my hut. However, when he decided to add a round-off into the middle splits and inadvertently destroyed my vanity, I knew I was stuck.

I had a new BFF named Upton.

"ARE YOU JUST GOING TO HANG AROUND ALL THE TIME?" I asked as Upton made an impressive sandcastle in the moonlight. "Don't you have a job? Or a family?"

Upton had followed me like a puppy since the moment I'd taken him on as a BFF. It was disconcerting and somewhat annoying to have a Pirate barnacle. Secretly it was wonderful. Although, when he tried to follow me to the bathroom, I zapped his ass and his breeches exploded into flames—my guess was that they were polyester. The royal-blue pantaloons went up like a firework. My BFF got the picture quick. He'd sprinted to the ocean to put the inferno out. To make up for the third-degree burns on his bottom, I conjured up a new pair of fire-retardant breeches in a nice red and navy plaid. Upton was thrilled.

"Me family is me crew and now the swimmin' hookers... I mean, Mermaids," Upton quickly corrected himself and backed away in case I made good on my threat to dropkick his scrawny butt a few miles out into the ocean. "Me and me crew will be lootin' a Target soon."

"You steal from Target?" I asked with a laugh.

"Aye," Upton said with an answering grin. "School for the wee bairns is startin' soon."

Tilting my head to the side, I stared at my new buddy. "Not following."

"Me and me sea farin' arses will loot pencils, notebooks, and glue sticks and then distribute to the wee bairns who be needin' them," he answered, settling his little body next to me in the sand.

"So, you're kind of like Robin Hood?" I inquired.

"Ye could say that," Upton agreed with a wink. "So why are ye leavin' the Mystical Isle, Petunia? Seems to me, yar cousins would be sad if ye left."

I had no answer for that, so I simply ignored the question—kind of.

"You know how on a cloudy night you can look up at the

sky and see a star in your peripheral vision? But when you try to look directly at the star it disappears?" I asked.

"Aye, lassie. I do," Upton said, nodding.

"I want to find that star. I need to find it."

"The one ye can't really see?" he asked.

"Yes, I want to see the star that won't let me look upon it. I feel like everything would be okay if I could finally see that star."

"What if the star isn't as pretty as ye might think it is?" Upton inquired, as he glanced up at the sky. "What if ye've been searchin' fer something that doesn't exist? What if everything ye need is right in front of ye already?"

His point wasn't lost on me. I'd considered it myself many times… especially lately.

"Ye know," Upton went on. "I've searched out many a hidden treasure in me time."

"You mean pilfered?" I asked with a raised brow trying to lighten the heavy conversation.

"Aye," Upton said with a cute giggle. "Semantics. But oftentimes the treasure isn't as precious as what's already in me life. Stars in the sky, gold nuggets, glue sticks and pilfered lawn furniture can't replace people."

I caught myself right before I almost called Upton *Dad*… My stomach clenched and my heart beat so quickly I was sure he could hear it. If he did, he made no comment. However, little did my BFF know his point only strengthened my resolve to leave.

"'Specially people like ye, Petunia," Upton added with a shy smile. "Ye is a wonderful lassie."

"Are you hitting on me, Upton?" I asked with a laugh. I

was fairly sure he wasn't, but I was hit on a lot. Sadly, the kind of guys who liked me were jerks... I was the Petunia the Mermaid: Loser Magnet.

"Nay, lassie!" Upton said with a belly laugh. "I have me own lovely wench. Love the violent she-devil to the moon and back."

"You have a mate?" I asked with interest. I'd almost had a mate once, but he disappeared just like everything else good in my life. If I ever laid eyes on the scoundrel again in my eternal lifetime, I'd drop-kick his sorry, good-looking, ridiculously sexy ass into the next century.

"Aye, I do," Upton said with a dreamy look on his adorably goofy face. "Met the scurvy harlot on an online datin' service run by the mighty and usually wasted god, Poseidon. Me tricorn-sportin' stern fouler of a gal almost beheaded me during our first round of courtin'. Good times. Good times."

I wasn't quite sure how to react to that, but Upton seemed to think his potential decapitation was normal. I'd just go with it. I mean, Mermaids were as violent as they came. A good knife fight or brawl was par for the course with us. Maybe Upton was into kinky stuff. After all, he did become one with his own nuts.

And *of course,* Poseidon ran a dating service on the side. He adored meddling in the affairs of those he cared about, and apparently, those he didn't as well. The perpetually soused, diaper-wearing leader of the sea population was every kind of insane. I loved him like the inebriated non-blood related grandfather he'd become to my cousins and me. The mossy green hair and Huggies were a little hard to take seriously, but the idiot usually meant well. And if a Pirate who could basically blow himself had found true love, well, maybe Poseidon was onto something.

"Your mate. Where is she?" I asked Upton, not sure if I wanted the answer but was too curious not to hear more.

"Yolanda is a Yeti," Upton whispered with a wide and delighted smile. "Me hairy little cackle fruit likes to mess with the humans who search for Big Foot on the telly. Yolanda has led them landlubbers on a chase for decades! Right now, she has over three hundred idiots trailing her delectable furry bottom."

Shaking my head, I laughed. It was perfect. Upton the nard licker was mated to Yolanda the furry-bottomed Yeti. I was sure she didn't mind his contortionist act. At least I hoped she didn't. Upton might be gross on the outside, but he was beautiful on the inside. Having him as a BFF didn't suck at all.

Shit.

I had to get out of here. In less than twenty-four hours I was becoming attached to a tiny little Pirate who could lick his bits, enjoyed looting chain stores and was besotted with a furry monster. Being with my cousins felt right and good which was terrible. Nothing good in my life had ever lasted. And if I stayed too long, it would be more devastating when it fell apart. I would *not* wear out my welcome.

Plus, everyone I came into contact with was happily mated—even Upton. It was freakin' depressing. Twenty-five years ago, the one man I thought was mine bolted just like everyone else had. Afterward, I'd determined that it had to be me. I was the problem. I knew I was stunning on the outside—all Mermaids were, but I clearly didn't have beautiful insides like my buddy Upton. People who were ugly inside didn't get happily ever afters.

So instead, I'd let the ocean current and the wind take me where it may. I knew nothing else. But what I did know was that the ocean had no power over me. I could live and let live without a care in the world.

However, it was also lonely and it sucked.

Here? I was beginning to care.

Not good.

I was like the star—my elusive star. The one that existed and no one could truly see. And that was how it had to be. Someday I would find that star and I would wish upon it. Someday... maybe I would find someone to love.

"Petunia?"

"Yes, Upton?" I replied. I was going to miss the little weirdo. He'd grown on me like a fungus in a very short period of time.

"Have ye ever been in love?" he asked.

Ahhh... how to answer. Since I was leaving, I figured the truth would be fine. Most likely I'd never see my scrawny little Pirate BFF again. "Once," I admitted. "He didn't want me."

Upton huffed in disgust. "Well then he's a thunderin', worm-riddled, fish gizzard. Ye don't need to be quaffin' or pining away for an arse like that. If I ever see the galley-hoppin', arthritic octopus, I'll put the hempin' halter on his disco stick and shove his head in the head."

I was pretty sure Upton had just promised castration

and a head flushing. It was all kinds of awesome. No one had looked out for me like this since my parents died.

"If I ever see him again, I'll be sure to let you know," I promised with a small smile as my heart hurt a bit. I'd thought I was over it.

"Mebbe ye should try Poseidon's online dating service," Upton suggested. "Ye never know. I'm the luckiest cutlass flappin' bilge drinker in the Universe to have found me Yolanda. Why don't ye stick around a wee bit longer and give it a try? Ye can find a bloke who will make yer heart pitter-patter. And if the scallywag treats ye wrong, I'll send the crab-infested dingly dangler to Davey Jones' locker."

Upton was making sense in a disgusting kind of way. Maybe putting myself out there was the thing to do. I'd never tried an online dating service. Part of me wanted to punch Upton in the head and part of me wanted to hug him. I did neither. I simply stared at the stars. It was a ridiculous notion, but if I was honest with myself, I didn't want to leave. This silliness would give me an excuse to stay on the Mystical Isle a little longer.

If Upton could find love, *mebbe* I could too.

2
DELPHINUS

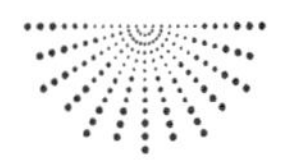

"So, let me get this straight," I said, making myself comfortable on the leather couch and propping my combat boot-clad feet on the desk of my annoyed and befuddled benefactor. "I get permanently sprung from the bottle if I agree to some ridiculous mission that the *elders* pull out of their asses?"

"Sure, sure, sure," Botein said without making eye contact.

Not good. My man Botein was a shitty liar.

Clearly while I'd been living it up in a tiny glass prison for a quarter of a century, 'ole Botein had moved up the Genie food chain. He had a swanky office in the main headquarters and was sporting the badge of the Genie Brigade. This turn of events was surprising. Things had definitely changed in twenty-five years.

Running my hands through my hair, I stood and accidentally on purpose shattered the bottle I'd been incarcerated in under my combat boot. Of course, Genie bottles were a dime a dozen. However, if I had to go back in, I wanted a new damned bottle.

"Define *sure, sure, sure,*" I said tersely.

"The parole requirements are being set by the elders," Botein answered as he rearranged all sorts of unrecognizable gadgets on his desk.

Well, that was alarming. The elders were asses and I'd done my time. I should be free and clear. "I'm on parole?"

"Umm... yes," Botein said with a long sigh. "You get sprung from the bottle, but if you so much as step out of line you'll be back in so fast your head will spin."

"Got it," I said, clenching my fists at my sides. It would be counterproductive to smackdown on Botein. Besides, I kind of liked him, or I used to before I did time. He was a bit of an uptight ass, but always up for a bourbon or three. I'd even asked the son of a bitch to be the witness to my mating—not that it ever got to happen. Nope, the slippery swimming gal of my dreams never showed up.

Whatever. That was seawater under a long-forgotten bridge.

Of course, brawling right after being released wasn't good form. Bad form was what landed me in the bottle in the first place. After I got stood up at the altar—so to speak, I went on a little tirade... of epic proportions. "I need specifics. The requirements?"

"I'm getting to that, Delphinus," Botein said with a wince.

"It's Del," I corrected him in a harsh tone. Only one person other than my mother was allowed to call me

Delphinus and she was dead to me. Now my certifiably insane, whack-job of a mother was alive and kicking and would call me Delphinus until the day I died, my light faded out or I was beheaded—whichever came first. The end result was the same. Thankfully, Genies were incredibly difficult to kill.

"Right. Del," Botein affirmed as he began to sweat.

Genies didn't sweat. What the hell was happening here?

"Interesting," I said, watching him carefully. Being human size again was delightful. If I needed to kick Botein's ass I was capable of doing it now. At full size, I was one of the deadliest Genies alive, or at least I was. A lot could have happened while I'd been hanging out in a fucking bottle. It had sucked being miniature for the last quarter of a century. "So please tell me you're not going to pull any of the three wishes bullshit?"

"I'm a Genie—like you, you idiot," Botein snapped as beads of perspiration flew from his upper lip. "Even if I wanted to force you to grant my wishes, I couldn't unless I wanted your sorry ass bound to me for all time. Didn't you learn anything in Djinn school?"

"Skipped a lot," I said with a grin. "Define *out of line*."

With an eye roll, Botein let his head hit the desk. Botein and I went way back—like two thousand years back. I hadn't always trusted him since he'd always been a bit of a *company man*, but I liked him right now for letting me out of the damned bottle. Hell, I'd agree to almost anything at this point, but I wasn't about to let him know that.

With his forehead pressed to the wood, he spoke. "No getting wasted and going on TV to prove that Genies do indeed exist. While we live somewhat openly, it gets rough when we get hunted down for wishes."

"Sounds fair," I replied with a chuckle. Had I actually done that? The time right before my bottled incarceration was a bit of a blur. I'd gotten quite chummy with aged bourbon since I was nursing a broken heart caused by a vicious, no-show, gorgeous, swimming she-devil. "Anything else?" I asked wondering what other unacceptable things I'd done.

"Stay off the booze. No stealing priceless art from museums and no streaking at televised sports events."

"Are you sure I did that?" I asked, my brow raised in surprise. Not really my style, but Botein was clearly reading from my rap sheet. My mother must have crapped her bejeweled harem pants.

"You did," he said, glancing up and shaking his head. "You're a fucking menace."

"Thank you."

"Wasn't a compliment."

"Yes," I replied dryly. "I know."

"Del, I'm serious here," Botein said, mopping the sweat from his forehead with a Genie Brigade monogrammed hanky. "I had to do some complicated tap dancing to get your reckless ass out—especially after the naked sprint during the Super Bowl. And then the art heist..."

Go big or go home had always been my motto. Clearly, I practiced what I preached. Even though I didn't remember it, I was impressed I'd chosen the Super Bowl. However, I did recall the art heist.

"Stealing the Mona Lisa was a dare from Pollux. Tell me you would have walked away from a dare—*from Pollux*."

"I can't tell you that, but Pollux is in a bottle now so you don't have him for an excuse," Botein replied.

"What did he do?" I asked, not the least bit surprised that Pollux was doing time.

"You didn't hear about it?"

"Nope. Been in a bottle for a while. No newspaper delivery there," I reminded him flatly.

"Right. My bad. Suffice it to say Pollux combined copious amounts of peach schnapps, a sequined bodysuit, genetically enhanced watermelons, a fifty-story building and a movie crew," Botein said with a shake of his head.

"He dropped watermelons off a fifty-story building?" I asked, impressed.

"He did… in New York City during the Thanksgiving Day Parade… and he filmed it. Extremely difficult and fucking expensive to get the NYPD off the case. Thankfully no one was injured except the creepy burger-slinging clown balloon. It was a messy shitshow. There was no way to save him. Pollux had been out of control for decades."

Glancing around Botein's office, I was slightly overwhelmed with all of the unfamiliar objects. His desk was covered with tiny machines—flat metal boxes with buttons. A strange sound came from a small handheld box that Botein swiped with his finger and then spoke into. My guess was that it was a phone but no cord was attached. Damn it, from the gadgets in his office, it appeared I'd missed quite a bit.

Touching the metal box again with his finger, he placed it carefully on his desk. His expression was grim.

"Umm… there's something I need to tell you," he said in a whisper, looking wildly uncomfortable.

"Spit it out," I replied flatly. I needed to get out of Genie headquarters immediately. Just being here was giving me hives.

"Your light is going out."

Shit.

That was an unwelcome and potentially life-threatening surprise. Glancing around wildly, I searched for a mirror. Genies were as vain as hell since we were all exceptionally good-looking bastards. Botein had to have a mirror or five.

The entire back wall of the office was floor to ceiling mirrors. Botein was indeed vain. Botein was also correct.

"Son of a bitch," I muttered as I stared at a dull version of myself. While my body looked the same, the sparkling Genie Star Fire Light in my eyes was muted and fading. What was happening to me? "I have to get out of here."

"You also have to get mated," Botein said, again with no eye contact. "To a Genie."

That command stopped me dead in my tracks.

"Repeat," I ground through clenched teeth.

No one in their right mind would mate with a female Genie. They were high maintenance, overly made up, seriously foul-mouthed, materialistic shrews. A full Genie didn't have to be born of two Genies. As long as the mother was a freakin' Genie the child was of the same race. My mother was definitely a Genie. Her mangled use of the English language had given me migraines for eons. I had a good idea who my father was and he was in no way a Genie. Male Genies did *not* mate with female Genies. That would be a shitshow far bigger than me showing my impressive nards and joystick at a football game. It would result in murder.

"For the past twenty-five years the elders have been concerned about the Genie race becoming watered down," Botein explained with a shudder of horror.

"So, *you* mated with a Genie?" I demanded.

"Umm... no," he admitted. "Still single."

"And alive," I mumbled.

"That too," Botein agreed, getting ready to duck if I decided to throw a punch.

"Yet it's been decided that I will mate with a Genie? This makes no sense," I growled as Botein seemed to shrink in his chair.

"You're the strongest Genie in existence," Botein pointed out as he slid lower and lower in the chair. "The elders feel you could be the beginning of creating Super Genies. Plus, if your Genie Star Fire Light is going out, getting offed by a female Genie might be a better way to go than a slow painful death."

Botein finished my epitaph on a terrified whisper. Tamping back my need to twist Botein into a pretzel and shove him into a bottle, I calmed myself with super inhuman effort. Reminding myself I'd just gotten out of the fucking bottle helped. However, the need to figure out what had happened to the light in my eyes is what really stopped me from shoving Botein's head up his pompous ass and pulling it out of his mouth.

"The elders can go fuck themselves," I shot back. "I'll go back to the bottle before I mate with a female Genie. I already found a mate."

"She didn't want you," Botein reminded me, staring at his shaking hands. "She changed the venue at the last moment and then didn't show up, Del. You have to get over her."

"I have," I lied easily although my gut churned.

Botein was incorrect. He'd clearly lost his mind along with his memory over the last quarter of a century. I supposed that working for the *elders* could do that to a Genie. *I'd* changed the venue because Botein had insisted that a Mermaid should be mated near the ocean. Clearly my romantic gesture had been rejected.

Old news.

However, I'd eat my magic carpet before I mated with a Genie. If I couldn't have the one who was meant for me, I would have no one at all. Besides, if my light went out, I was a goner anyway.

"Am I free to leave?" I questioned an increasingly nervous Botein.

"You are," he replied cautiously. "Just keep in mind what I have told you."

Narrowing my eyes at the man whom I used to call friend, I shrugged and smiled. "Will do."

With a snap of my fingers, my magic carpet appeared and floated in the air next to me. I'd missed my old friend. Settling myself comfortably on the plush fabric, I felt a little bit of my old self come back. However, the calming feeling was brief.

I had a horrifying visit to make.

It would be unpleasant, but it had to be done. I shuddered at the thought of seeing my mother and listening to the riot act about displaying my ass and assets on national television. But if my light was fading, she would know what to do.

At least I hoped she would.

I'd just gotten out of the bottle. It wasn't my week to die.

"Hello Mother. Long time no see," I said, wanting to quickly get past the elephant in the room of my jail time. "I might have a bit of a problem and I was hoping you could help me."

Glancing around her enormous living room, I remembered her garish taste. Every surface was covered in jewels and lush velvets—very typical Genie décor.

It made me itch.

"*Everyone* has problems, Happy Camel Mango. Most of us don't have to spend a quarter of a century in a bottle because of them." She raised a perfectly plucked eyebrow at me and went on. "Do these harem pants make my tushy look fat, Sparkling Cupcake Penguin?" my mother inquired while modeling a hideous looking getup covered in so many sparkling rubies and emeralds I had to magically produce sunglasses.

Holy hell, I'd forgotten how much I *loved* her emasculating pet names. My mother, Adara, was as generous with mortifying nicknames for me as she was with insults about everyone else.

There was one clear answer to my mother's question and it wasn't the truth. "You look lovely," I lied through my teeth. Being set on fire wasn't on my agenda today so I went with the safe answer.

"Thank you, Jolly Pancake Llama," she squealed. "Spica and the rest of the pie-eating crotch knobs in my basket weaving class will be green with envy at my sparkle!"

"That's umm... fantastic," I muttered with a wince. The visual she'd created was almost enough to make me hop back on my carpet and ride like the wind.

Almost.

My mother glanced at herself in one of the many mirrors in her lavish sitting room. She smiled and blew herself a kiss. It was all I could do not to laugh or groan. No one loved my mother as much as she loved herself.

No one.

I loved her mostly because she was my mother. However, I only liked her on the rare occasion. Hopefully, today would be one of those occasions.

"I know you're fibbing, Delphinus my little Yummy Gummy Bear," she replied, snapping her fingers and magically replacing the unattractive jeweled ensemble with a more slimming pair of black harem pants and a sequined boob tube. "I need to get the butt implants removed. I just can't seem to find the time to do it. J. Lo's ass is so last week. Right?"

There was no reply that wouldn't get me zapped into

next year. I shrugged and smiled—hoping my smile didn't look like a constipated wince.

"So, how has the last quarter of a century been treating you, Mother?" I inquired politely, making small talk before I got back down to business.

Her eyes narrowed dangerously and her blond locks began to blow around her head. Small talk was a bad idea.

"Well, Dirty Apple Pie Flamingo," she huffed as she seated herself on a diamond-covered chaise and positioned herself with her best side showing. "Let's see, I spent ten years explaining to my hamster-humping, crap-faced bridge club why you thought displaying your danglies on national television was a fine idea. Although, yours are far larger than any of their sons' bits."

"Thank you," I said, letting my head fall back on my shoulders and closing my eyes. Coming here was a bad plan. However, I didn't have another one at the moment.

"You're welcome, Dazzling Blueberry Ferret," she said. "You get those big balls from your father. Literally. His balls are bigger than his brain. You also got your drinking problem from him."

"I don't have a drinking problem," I snapped.

"Says the Genie who displayed his salami at the Super Bowl."

"Fine point. Well made," I admitted. However, she was wrong—not that I would tell her. I rarely imbibed. It was my injured pride and broken heart that had gone on a bender. Never again.

"All your bad habits come from your shart hound of a father. I'm perfect," she announced.

"Speaking of, would you like to confirm who he is?" I questioned, not about to touch the balls intel.

Ignoring my request—as usual—she went on.

"I have a facelift, Botox and filler appointment in an hour. After that I'm getting my nether regions waxed and then I'm having my palm read. I'm certain this isn't a social visit since you never visit me. What is it that you want, Delphinus?"

After that bizarre and distasteful diatribe, I'd almost forgotten why I'd come. "You're immortal," I reminded my mother. "Why are you having plastic surgery?"

"Pish," she said with a wave of her expertly manicured hand. "It's fun. Fish lips are all the rage. I'll look fabu! Vega, my online Scrabble partner who cheats, got a set. I need to one-up that lazy boner clown."

Gods, I'd hate to see the words they came up with for Scrabble. The conversation was degenerating quickly. I needed to get to the heart of the matter immediately.

"Right," I said, removing my sunglasses and staring at my mother.

Her gasp was not music to my ears. Part of me was hoping Botein had been wrong about my light going out and that my mother wouldn't notice.

"Sweet Goddess Genie Barbra Eden on a bender," she shrieked so loudly several of her mirrors shattered. "What has happened to you?"

She noticed. Shit was serious.

"Did those scum-sipping, boner-camper *elders* do this to you when you were in the glass pokey?" she demanded as she began to levitate and spark. "I *despise* those pie-eating sphincter waffles."

"Not as far as I know," I replied, ducking a glittering zap of fire that flew from her fingers. I suppose if she got angrier, I'd die by fireball this afternoon and not have to worry about my Genie light going out. I'd been borne of a certifiable nut-job. It might be fitting if she took me out as well. At this point I didn't have much to live for anyway.

"I will call on those crap-banging nose farmers and make them sopranos for harming my Sugar Lump Monkey. They will rue the day they were hatched," she hissed as small shimmering silver and golden fires broke out all over her mansion.

"You might want to tamp that shit back, Mom," I said, quickly jumping out of the line of fire. Literally.

"Sorry, Happy Iguana Kiwi," she said, waving her hand and dousing the flames. "You must go to your father. The butterfaced bitch-goblin will know what to do."

"Why will my father know what to do?" I asked, frustrated. "He's not a Genie."

"No," she agreed. "He's not. He's a frilly rectum canoe along with being a *god*."

"So I was right about the identity of my father?" I demanded, both relieved and horrified.

"I'll give you three guesses, Squishy Popsicle Hedgehog," she said with her right brow raised so high I thought it might reach her hairline.

"Does he wear a diaper?" I asked.

"Yes."

"Carry a scepter?"

"Yes."

"Is known as an idiot all over the Immortal Universe?"

"Yes."

Fuck. My next stop was Mount Olympus to see my father… Poseidon.

3
PETUNIA

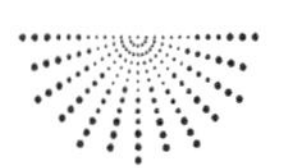

"OKAY, HERE'S THE DEAL," TALLULAH ANNOUNCED WITH HER lavender locks blowing ominously around her head as she stood in the doorway of my hut. "If you leave, we're coming after you."

"And we'll kick your ass," Madison added with a grin.

"With love. We'll kick your ass with love," Ariel was quick to chime in with a giggle.

"I mean, it'll hurt like a mother humper, but it will definitely be in the name of love," Misty finished off with gusto.

"You think you could take me?" I inquired with a wide smile. It tickled me how violent my sea-loving family was.

"Four on one," Madison explained with a wink. "Odds are on our side."

She did have a point. I was a maniac, but they were certifiable.

With the sun shining bright behind my cousins, they looked like avenging crayons with fantastic figures and fabulous boobs. Of course, I fit right into the crayon box. Mermaids had very specific traits.

Our hair and our eyes were set from birth. My color was orange. Madison's color was pink, Ariel's was blue, Misty's was emerald green and Tallulah's was lavender. Each Mermaid's hair and eyes were unique to them and no two were alike. However, the color of our tails changed with our moods and our fashion choices. I always matched my tail—or when in human form, my sarong skirt—to my bikini top.

"Not to mention, Upton will be devastated if you leave," Tallulah pointed out. "Right, Upton?"

"Aye," Upton agreed, grinning as he dusted my hut and picked up my dirty sarongs. "Me little Petunia is a delight. Yolanda is gonna love her. Plus, Petunia is gonna join the online dating site! We're gonna find her an upstandin' scally-wag. And if the tar stain treats me little swimmer bad, I'll send the crab-infested dingly dangler to Davey Jones' locker."

"Maybe," I said with an eye roll as my cousins' ears perked up.

"I think it's a great idea!" Ariel said, clapping her hands together. "Which dating site are you going to use?"

"There's more than one?" I asked, confused as I glanced over at Upton.

"Nay," Upton told the group. "Me little Mermaid is going to use the same site that I met me cackle fruit, Yolanda, on. It's the one Poseidon runs."

"Holy hell and seashells," Madison said with a belly laugh. "Our de facto, drunk, non-related pappy has an online dating service?"

"Makes sense," Misty said. "He meddles more than an old lady. It's perfect."

The talk made me nervous. This was a bad idea. Poseidon was an idiot. I mean, I loved him, but he was a diaper-wearing dolt. I could find dumbasses on my own. I didn't need help from the God of the Sea.

"What's the site called?" Tallulah asked.

Upton blanched and shook his head. That *did not* bode well. The Pirate thought licking his nards was acceptable. The name had to be *bad*.

"Well," he said with great hesitation. "Poseidon wanted to call it Immortal Match."

"Isn't there already an Immortal Match?" Ariel asked.

"Aye. They sued him somethin' terrible," Upton said. "So, the soused dumbarse went with umm... another name. Ye know... somethin' similar."

"The name?" I requested again with great trepidation.

"Immortal Snatch," Upton whispered.

"It's called Immortal *Snatch*?" I shouted, not knowing whether to laugh or blow something up. "He named a dating service Immortal *Snatch*? That's disgusting."

"It really is." Ariel scrunched her nose and tried not to laugh.

She failed.

"Very... umm... descriptive," Madison said, not hiding her mirth at all.

"Well, we *are* talking about Poseidon," Tallulah pointed out. "His balls are bigger than his brains."

"You've seen his balls?" Misty asked on a gag.

"NO," Tallulah shouted. "I'd be blind if I'd ever seen his junk. It's just the rumor on the High Seas."

"Aye," Upton said, turning green-ish. "Tis true."

"You've seen his gangoolies?" I asked, shocked and appalled.

Upton nodded and shuddered.

"And you lived?" I pressed.

"Upton's a Sphinx," Tallulah informed me. "It would take more than an oversized set of wrinkly god nards to kill a Sphinx."

"Well, I'll be damned," I said, glancing over at my BFF with new admiration. I'd always believed the Sphinx were myth. I thought back to our earlier conversation and shook my head. I'd punched a Sphinx… and lived.

My BFF and I had our first disagreement earlier over my housekeeping skills. Upton thought I had none. I'd punched him in the head and he just laughed like a loon. The little Pirate then pointed out all my faults while using examples. Amazingly, he was correct. I was a slob.

Turned out Upton liked to clean—said it relaxed him. I felt kind of guilty about that so I suggested a trade. I made killer chocolate chip seaweed cookies and promised him a weekly batch. Upton squealed like a girl and did an outstanding cheerleader herkie jump. Chocolate chip seaweed cookies were his favorite. I felt better about myself when Upton admitted that he burned water. It wasn't exactly a fair trade since Upton got the raw end of the deal, but he seemed very happy.

"Umm… sorry about slugging you in the face earlier."

"Nay, lassie," Upton said gleefully. "I deserved it for callin' ye a slob."

"But I am a slob," I reminded him.

"That ye are," he said with a grin and continued to clean.

Leave it to me to wallop a Sphinx who can do a herkie jump.

"I'd also like to have it go on official record that since becoming your BFF, Upton hasn't licked his nards in public," Misty said with a thumbs up to the Pirate.

All four of my cousins broke into applause for my scrawny BFF. Basking in his adoration, Upton grinned and slid in the splits while continuing to dust. The Pirate-Sphinx was talented.

"I would like to thank you for that miracle, Petunia," Ariel said with a giggle. "I just finished taking care of a lawsuit with a human guest family who were traumatized by Upton's limber hobbies."

"Sorry about that," Upton said, turning pink in the face.

"No worries," Ariel told him and kissed the top of his head. "I think they were jealous. Plus, the father ended up in traction trying to have a go at his own pork sword."

"So, anyhoo," Tallulah went on, marching into my hut and making herself comfortable. "As you can plainly see, running a tourist trap for humans in the middle of the Bermuda Triangle comes with a unique set of challenges. We could *really* use your help here, Petunia."

With a roll of my eyes, I sighed and then laughed. My cousins wouldn't give up until I'd firmly planted roots right next door to them. It made my tail tingle with happiness and dread. Reminding myself that I was bad luck, I got ready to make up something semi-plausible about why I had to leave.

"First of all," I said, helping Upton get out of the splits. "I'm not really good at much besides partying and killing stuff. My skill set doesn't actually help in any kind of legal business."

"Actually, it might," Madison said, glancing warily over at her sisters who nodded for her to continue. "We have an issue that needs to be eliminated."

"The issue?" I inquired, wondering what they'd come up with this time. My family had been concocting bullshit reasons for me to stay for weeks.

"Whirlpools," Madison said with a shudder. "Deadly whirlpools have started developing in the water around the Mystical Isle."

My gut clenched in fury and my fingertips began to shoot bright orange sparks. My parents had died in a toxic magical whirlpool. I'd seen it happen with my own eyes. We'd been swimming happily in the ocean on a gorgeous starlit evening and then next thing I knew, I was being thrown a mile away from the fatal tragedy. With his last bit of strength, my father grabbed me and hurled me away from the poisonous maelstrom.

I'd swam back like Hades himself was on my tail to where my parents were dying, but I was too late. My father's last act in this world had been to save me. Sadly, I knew I wasn't worth saving. I'd amounted to little more than a party Mermaid with an aptitude for terminating bad dudes and dudettes. I'd never mated—never given them little swimming grandbabies. I didn't even have a home for the love of the Goddess and no career to speak of either. I should have died with them.

I'd pretty much failed at immortal life. But then again, immortal meant forever.

Maybe I could turn the frown my life had become upside down. Was this a sign? A gift?

Had the time arrived for me to avenge their deaths? I'd searched for a century to find out what had caused the whirlpool and had no luck.

"Has anyone died?" I ground out. I knew my eyes were blazing orange. Everything in my line of vision appeared bathed in fire.

"Not yet," Tallulah said, not backing up an inch even though I was pretty dang sure I was quite scary at the moment. "There have been a few close calls. We've had to close down the beaches for swimming."

"Guests have canceled in droves," Misty added.

"Do you have any idea what or who is causing it?" I asked, tamping back my magic so I didn't blow up the hut with all the people I cared about inside it.

I knew everyone would survive an explosion because we were immortal. But it sucked having to heal from fire—itched like a mother humper. Plus, my hut was clean for the first time in weeks. It would be a dang shame to mess it up.

"Not a clue," Tallulah said, shaking her head in frustration.

"Well, if ye violent lassies want me humble opinion, I'd have to say it sounds like the bandana wearin' pantaloon splinter that me and the arses have come across a few times while sailing the Seven Seas on our pilfering tours. The shite's a fake-bearded crab-infested rockpool if ye ask me," Upton said, seating himself next to Tallulah and looking quite serious.

"Can you repeat that in English?" I asked, not wanting to offend my BFF, but I had no clue what he'd just said.

"Certainly," Upton said. "The cutlass flappin' fish stink is a black spot in the dungbie. Ate our powder monkey, Winwood 'No Smile' Camden. Now, no one liked that ole seadog Winwood, but it was a bad way to feed the fish. The Old Salt got sucked down in the worm riddled fish gizzard whirlpool never to be heard from again."

All of us were confused now. Well, everyone except Upton.

"Mmkay," I said, trying to figure out another way to get the information I needed. "What was the cutlass flappin' fish stink called? Did it have a name?"

"Oh," Upton said with a giggle. "Yar should have just asked. It's called Charybdis—meanest monster of the sea. Rumor has it the shite-stinkin' frigate-eatin' riffraff started on a rampage about a century ago."

The timing was right. My parents had been killed a hundred years ago. I could feel excitement mixed with sadness and rage burning in my gut.

"We need to tell Poseidon," Tallulah said, standing up. "Immediately."

"Nope," I insisted, grabbing her hand to stop her. "Charybdis is mine. I'm sure she's the monster who killed my parents. Plus, Poseidon would screw it up. You think someone who named a dating service *Immortal Snatch* is capable of good ideas in how to eliminate a lethal problem?"

"She has a point," Ariel said.

"I'm *really* good at killing shit," I volunteered.

"She is," Madison chimed in. "Petunia took the evil Gnomes out with a freakin' finger flick."

"Impressive," Tallulah said, twisting her lavender hair in her fingers as she thought. "But, if memory serves, I seem to recall learning back in school that Charybdis is a daughter of Poseidon. Of course, he had over a thousand children."

Well, that was news. Bad news. And all the more reason Poseidon should not be involved.

For the first time in a century other than when I was *supposed* to be mated, I felt hopeful. I felt like I could make a real difference. I could avenge the people I loved from my past while keeping the people I loved right now safe.

Win. Win.

Maybe, if I did something for others, I would finally find my elusive star.

"I have to do this," I told Tallulah. "You have to let me."

"Will you stay then?" Tallulah asked, watching me closely. "For good?"

Nodding before I'd even processed what she had said, I realized it was what I wanted. If I couldn't have the whole package of a happily ever after, I could at least have the happy part. The Mystical Isle felt like more of a home to me than any other place had since my parents were alive. The people who loved me—warts and all—were right here.

"I'll stay. And I'll join Immortal Snatch," I said with a shudder. "Not to find a man though. Men suck. Well, not Upton, but other ones, or at least the ones who like me. I'll join it so I can grill Poseidon about Charybdis. It's a perfect cover."

"Me Petunia is beautiful and smart!" Upton announced with pride. "Ye will be careful. Yolanda will kick me arse if somethin' happens to ye."

"She doesn't even know me," I told him.

"She knows all about ye," Upton said with a sly smile. "And she already loves ye like I do."

I was unsure how to react so I didn't. I wasn't really all that lovable. All the love being showered on me was uncomfortable, but it also felt wonderful. Maybe I didn't need to see the star after all. Maybe Upton was right. All I needed was right here in front of me.

Now I just needed to keep them safe.

I HAD THE IDIOT ON SPEED DIAL. HE ANSWERED ON THE FIRST ring.

"I want to join Immortal Snatch," I said into my cell phone as my cousins tried not to laugh.

"*What's wrong with your snatch?*" Poseidon asked, confused.

"Nothing is wrong with my snatch, you idiot," I shouted into the phone as Tallulah fell off her chair in hysterics. "I want to register for your heinously named dating service."

"*Oh, I thought you said you wanted to coin your snatch—didn't know what that meant,*" Poseidon said.

"How much rum have you had?" I demanded with an eye roll.

"Started at nine AM," he replied. *"You would have too if you were me. DIC is killing me."*

"Did he just say his dick is killing him?" Ariel whispered as she choked on a laugh.

Nodding my head, I rolled my eyes. "That is far too much information, old man," I snapped into the phone. "You're like a drunk non-blood related grandfather to me that I wouldn't take out in public. I do not want to know about your salami. You feel me, dumbass?"

"Not my dick," Poseidon yelled with a bellow of laughter. *"DIC."*

"Well, that certainly clears it up—not," I grumbled.

"DIC—as in Divine Immortal Circuit. All the gods have to take a turn at governing the other idiot gods, demigods and lesser gods. I lost at strip poker a few months back and have to run the damned thing for the next hundred years."

"Well, umm... okay then," I said, letting my chin drop to my chest. "So, can I join?"

"DIC?" Poseidon asked, confused again.

"Umm, no. I want nothing to do with DIC," I replied.

"So, you're a lesbian now?" he asked politely.

It took all I had not to throw my phone into the ocean. But wait... the diapered idiot had given me an opening. Possibly.

"Well... umm... not exactly, but I was wondering if your daughter Charybdis was enrolled," I said, holding my breath.

Upton gave me a thumbs up for my quick and creative thinking. It warmed me all over to have his approval. All four of my cousins' eyes grew wide and they began to bounce up and down on my couch.

"I disowned that shrew thousands of years ago," Poseidon grunted with disgust. *"That murdering sea wench is no longer my daughter. And if you are going to the gay side, I'd like to suggest a less homicidal muff diver."*

"That was politically incorrect," I told him with a sigh of exasperation. However, I was delighted that if I offed Charybdis he wouldn't be put out.

"Which part?" Poseidon asked.

"Most of it," I replied.

"My bad. My whole life is politically incorrect. So, should I be looking for a man or a woman for you?"

"Doesn't matter," I said honestly. I had no intention of actually going on a date with anyone.

"What is it that you're looking for, Petunia?" Poseidon asked kindly.

Without thinking, I told the God of the Sea the truth. "A star," I said. "I want to wish on a star."

"Tall order there, little flame-haired Mermaid," Poseidon said with a laugh. *"I'll get to work on it."*

Hanging up, I sighed and then pasted a smile on my lips for my cousins and Upton.

There was no way in hell Poseidon could give me what I wanted, god or no. I'd almost had my star, but he had disappeared just like all the good things in my life had. But that was about to change. The Mystical Isle was my new home. My cousins were my family. I adored them. And Upton? Upton was my new dad. I'd never tell him so, but it was magical to pretend.

"Okay," I said, slapping my hands onto my hips. "It's time to find a sea monster."

"If it doesn't find us first," Tallulah said.

"Not to worry," I promised. "I'm feeling lucky today."

Famous last words…

4
DELPHINUS

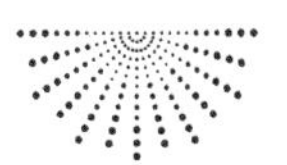

"Delphinus, good to see you!" Poseidon bellowed as he produced a bottle of rum from his diaper and offered me a swig.

Holding up my hand and schooling my face to a neutral expression took everything I had. As much as I wouldn't mind some alcoholic courage at the moment, I refused to partake from a bottle that had been stored next to his junk. Not to mention, I wanted to smackdown on him for being my father. The fact that he knew who I was surprised me.

It wasn't as if I hadn't suspected it was him. My powers were much stronger than a normal male Genie—not that we were all that *normal* to begin with. The female Genies were far more magical. A male Genie had the power of seduction and the power to grant wishes. That was about it. I, on the other hand, could kick ass with magic like a champion and I swam like a damned dolphin. I was the deadliest Genie alive. Well, alive at the moment.

"Going by Del now... *Dad,*" I corrected the certifiable God of the Sea in a rude tone glancing around his grossly ornate office.

"So, your mom finally let the cat out of the bag," Poseidon said with a grin.

"More like the shitass out of the suitcase," I said flatly.

"That works too," Poseidon said, still grinning like an idiot.

It was difficult to take him seriously in a diaper. His long mossy green hair was dated and out of style, but I had to admit a tiny part of me was excited to be in his presence. However, that was information I wasn't planning to share. He'd had two thousand years to show up and never had.

"Sooooo, Del," Poseidon went on as if I wasn't staring daggers at him. "How's your mother?"

"Fine. She refers to you as a butterfaced bitch-goblin," I told him.

His raucous laughter almost made me smile, but not quite.

"Nice to hear she hasn't changed," he said with a chuckle and a shudder. "And while I'm relieved as hell that your mother wasn't my true mate, it was very enjoyable procreating with her. Of course, I was drunk but that doesn't make me any less proud of you."

"I'd have to disagree," I shot back. "You haven't shown up for me. Ever."

"Tis true," Poseidon agreed, shaking his head sadly. "Adara threatened to dismember me and feed my magnificent Johnson to the sharks if I did. I believe her parting words were 'You stupid nut biscuit. I never should have boinked a thighbone hugging toilet zoo like you. However, I got my beautiful boy and if you ever come near him, I'll make you a grandpa humping cork vendor—a dead one'."

I had to admit that sounded exactly like my mother. Her way of turning a profane phrase was horrifyingly recognizable.

"Wow," was I could muster up to that. I'd have stayed away too. My mother was lethal when pissed off.

Poseidon took a healthy swig off his bottle and winked at me. I wasn't sure if I wanted to punch him or hug him. I decided to do neither. I still needed his help.

"Now that we've cleared up my necessary absence in your life due to the longevity of my pecker, you can call me Pappy," the idiot announced.

"I'm going to stick with butterfaced bitch-goblin for the time being," I told him as I relaxed my stance and took a seat in a chair made of giant clamshells.

His office was just as appalling and over-the-top as my mother's home—in a more ocean-themed way. The sand on the floor was positively inspired and was going to be stuck in the grooves of my combat boots for weeks.

"I answer to anything," Poseidon assured me as he shuffled through papers on his massive sea glass desk. "Butter-faced bitch-goblin is far more pleasant than the names my mate Wally comes up with."

Before I could stop my mouth from blurting out what I was thinking, I asked a question I really didn't want the answer to. "You're gay?"

Poseidon was mid-slug on his rum and spit it all over his desk as he choked and laughed. I was slightly concerned I'd have to Heimlich him, but thankfully he pulled himself back together. "Nay, I'm as straight as my enormous pecker. Wally happens to be a woman, but I'd love the old bag no matter what sex she was—horrible, horrible vile piece of work, but great in the sack. But I have no problem with the muff divers and the butt men."

I winced in pain at my father's lack of political correctness. He was clearly known as an idiot all over the immortal Universe for a reason.

"That was every kind of wrong," I said, shaking my head. "You should probably speak less."

"Tell me about it," Poseidon moaned. "I can't keep up with the lingo—got no time. DIC is killing me."

Letting my chin fall to my chest, I sighed. Maybe it would be better to die. If I was going to turn out like my mother or Gods forbid, my father, I didn't have much to look forward to. The only orange-haired, she-devil of a woman I'd ever loved didn't want me. Clearly, she was smart. I came from dubious parentage.

"Well, if you're having dick issues, you should probably see a doctor about that," I said stiffly, thinking this might be the right time to get the hell out.

My pappy's roar of laughter made me realized how truly insane or drunk he was. Why my mother thought he could help was beyond me.

"Not my Johnson! DIC—Divine Immortal Circuit. I'm in charge of all the halfwit gods for the next century—bunch of whiny little shites," he explained, still chuckling. "And by the way, your salami is impressive. Saw it twenty-five years ago when you streaked across the fifty-yard line at the

Super Bowl. Made me proud, son. Thank Zeus' saggy ass, I videotaped the game. I check out your inherited package once a month. Makes me feel closer to you since your mom wouldn't let me near you."

I was speechless. I didn't know whether to be horrified or delighted. To be honest, I was a little of both. I needed therapy.

"It was painfully great meeting you. I have to go," I said and stood to leave.

"Ya know," he went on, ignoring me. "You're not the only one who thinks my way with words needs help. One of my favorite little swimming hookers, Petunia, said the same thing to me just an hour ago. I love that savage little gal like a daughter."

That stopped me dead in my tracks. My head whipped up and I glared at the butterfaced bitch-goblin. I hadn't heard that particular name in twenty-five years. I refused to speak it. She'd ruined my life and sent me to the pokey.

Actually, I could take all the credit for ending up in a glass prison. Petunia had nothing to do with me drinking myself into a stupor and displaying my goods. Well, not directly.

"I'm sorry," I choked out as Poseidon watched me with great interest. "Could you repeat yourself?"

"Which part?" he inquired with a grin on his face that I didn't like.

"The name. Say the name again," I growled.

"Petunia?" he asked, looking as innocent as a whack-job could. "Do you know her?"

"I used to," I snapped and then flopped back down onto

the uncomfortable chair. "How is she?"

"Rude as ever," Poseidon replied. "Asked to join Immortal Snatch."

"Something is wrong with her snatch?" I asked, unable to fathom what my *pappy* had just volunteered. On top of that, I couldn't believe I'd just spoken the word *snatch.*

"Nay," he said. "I asked her the same question. Forgot I'd named my dating service after Wally's hooha. Caught me off guard. Anyhoo, I think she's gay."

This was too much to take in. I was dying and my former love was now a lesbian who joined a dating service called *Immortal Snatch?*

"Do you mind if I punch you in the head?" I asked my father politely. "I feel the need to hit something and I'd love to take my frustration out on your face."

Poseidon didn't miss a beat. "Hit me, boy! You deserve to throw a few left hooks at your pappy. It must have sucked not having a father—not that I'm a good father. Having over a thousand children is problematic. Not enough time in the day with all my DIC issues."

"You realize that was a fucking awful pun. Right?" I said as I crossed the room and got ready to wail on the God of the Sea.

"Well, there you go. I'm smarter than I look," Poseidon said triumphantly. "I'm gonna hit back. You good with that?"

"I'd expect no less," I said with a grin as I reared back and nailed him between the eyes with a right jab that sent him flying.

I felt the hit vibrate all the way up my arm to my shoulder. The man's head was hard. It was life-changing to be able to let loose and smackdown on someone knowing I wouldn't kill him. My butterfaced bitch-goblin of a father was a god. Gods were impossible to kill.

Best day of my life.

Pappy came back with an uppercut that made me see stars. Of course, my one-two punch made him grunt and then scream like a girl.

Game was on. I hadn't had this much fun in centuries.

"You hit like a freight train," Poseidon said with pride as he mopped the blood from his forehead.

"You're not so bad yourself for an old man," I replied, squinting at him through my almost swollen shut eyes.

The fight had lasted thirty glorious minutes. His office looked like a tsunami had rolled through. I had sand in every orifice, but I didn't care. The feeling of freedom was intoxicating. Several times I was sure I was dead but got back to my feet with super inhuman effort. My father was a worthy opponent. Insane but worthy.

Poseidon pulled a fresh bottle of rum from a drawer in his desk and tossed it to me. "The bottle in my diaper busted when you dropkicked me across the room. Now I actually might have real dick problems."

I was no longer able to play it cool with the dolt. I let my head fall back on my shoulders and I laughed. For real. The man was certifiable. And his rum was excellent.

"So, Del, why are you here? I mean, I'm glad you are," he

said quickly. "I haven't had an ass-kicking like that in centuries. Always afraid if I really let loose, I'll kill someone."

"Same," I said, taking another swig and then handing him the bottle. "My mother said I should come see you about a little problem I'm having."

"Spit it out, boy. I'm an excellent life coach," he boasted.

That was highly unlikely but I had nothing to lose... except my life.

"You're aware the Genies are stars, right? Each one of us is an actual star," I told him, hoping I wouldn't have to educate him on my kind.

"Yep."

"And if the Genie Star Fire Light in our eyes fades out, we die," I continued.

"Yep."

His one-word answers weren't exactly what I was hoping for.

"My light is going out. I don't know why. My mother thinks the Genie elders have something to do with it."

"That certainly explains the report I got earlier," Poseidon said with a laugh. "There's been a smackdown at Genie headquarters. Apparently, a vicious female Genie went apeshit crazy and put the entire elder community into bottles."

Gods, I really did love my mother.

"So, Adara thinks I can help you with the Genie Star Fire Light in your eyes?" Poseidon asked with an odd expression on his battered face.

"Can you?"

The answer was probably no, but I had to admit if I was headed out of this world it was nice to have met my pappy.

"You ready to follow orders and not ask questions?" Poseidon asked as he downed the rest of the rum in the bottle and went for another.

He raised a bushy green eyebrow and waited for my answer. Like I really had a choice here?

"Can I hit you if I think it's bullshit as long as I don't question your wisdom or lack thereof?"

"Absolutely, boy! I was hoping you'd want to go another round," he shouted and got to his feet.

Pushing myself to a standing position with effort, I grinned and got ready to go at him again. "Orders?" I demanded as I fisted my hands and got into a fighting stance.

"Your light is going out because you found your true mate and left her," Pappy announced as he expertly dodged the vicious right hook I threw at his head.

"I didn't leave her. She didn't want me," I roared as I avoided the clamshell chair he hurled at me in retaliation. "Besides, Genies don't have true mates."

"You're not just a Genie," Poseidon announced as he threw a bolt of lightning that almost singed the hair off my head. "Take a look in the mirror, son, you have the salami of a GOD!"

And that's when I laughed. Biggest mistake of the day so far. Pappy got an excellent left hook in that sent me flying and tumbling into his sea glass desk. It shattered into a million glittering shards. If I wasn't immortal, I'd have been sliced to shreds.

"Well then," I said, crawling back to my feet and brushing the sparkling glass off my clothes. "I guess I'm a goner."

"You'd be guessing wrong," Poseidon shot back, grabbing a flat metal rectangle that had somehow avoided getting smashed in the melee. "Get your violent ass over here. You're the newest member of Immortal Snatch."

"What's that in your hands?" I asked, holding back the need to take him down again.

"It's a laptop computer," Poseidon replied. "It's a real pain in the ass, but I enjoy playing online Scrabble on it. Pretty sure your mother is playing online too. There is some awful language going on in that chat room."

"Probably," I agreed as I watched him type rapidly on a keyboard that produced pictures on a screen. I'd missed a lot of technology while I'd been in the bottle.

"You'll be headed to Mystical Isle soon," he said, snapping the box shut and grinning from ear to ear.

"What's on Mystical Isle?" I asked warily, feeling my heart beat wildly in my chest.

Poseidon swallowed the entire contents of his new bottle of rum and then burped like a champion. "Your Genie Star Fire Light is there, boy. And you also have a brother living there named Pirate Doug that will help you. He's an arse, but he's blood."

"It's that easy?" I asked doubtfully.

"Nothing is easy," my father said. "Not a damned thing worth anything is easy."

Those had been the wisest words he spoken so far.

Unfortunately, he was correct. Very correct.

5
PETUNIA

IT HAD BEEN FIVE DAYS OF NON-STOP SEARCHING FOR Charybdis and I'd come up empty every time. The whirlpools were everywhere, but there was no sign of the deadly sea monster.

"She has to be near or the whirlpools wouldn't be increasing," I grunted in frustration as I flopped down on the couch in my hut.

"Aye, I believe the stripey-sweatered sea snake is in the area. Charybdis'll show her arse soon. Monsters like that one like the credit for thar weevil-eatin' dastardly deeds," Upton said, digging into his batch of chocolate chip seaweed cookies with gusto. "Do ye think ye could make an extra batch so I can send some to me cackle fish?"

"Yolanda likes cookies?" I asked.

"Aye, little lassie. Me Yolanda has a sweet tooth. Me gal ate the entire dessert aisle in Target last time I was there doin' me pilferin'. It was a sight to see—just beautiful."

The picture in my head wasn't exactly flattering, so I kept my thoughts to myself. Upton enjoyed licking his nards and Yolanda could eat her own weight in sweets. What did I expect? Honestly though, I couldn't wait to meet her. As crazy as the stories that Upton told about his mate, she sounded truly lovely—albeit covered in hair and cookie crumbs.

"Yep, I made some extra. Do you have an address to send them?" I asked, grabbing a few dozen.

"Don't need one," Upton said with a giggle as he snapped his fingers and the cookies disappeared in a pop of icy blue magic. "Me furry love will get them much faster this way than the post office."

Gods, I adored magic.

"Okay, we're here," Tallulah announced as she and my cousins marched into my hut and made themselves at home.

It was odd getting used to having the same people as a constant in my life and I loved it—cautiously. For the first time in a very long time, I felt at home.

"And why are you here?" I asked with a grin as I grabbed another plate of cookies and put them on the sea glass coffee table.

"We have to get you registered on *Immortal Snatch*," Misty said with a wink as she went for a cookie.

"Nope. Not doing it. The only reason I said I would was to get info on Charybdis from Poseidon. Since she's been disowned there's nothing to learn."

Madison pulled a laptop out of her beach bag and snapped it open. "I disagree. Plus, Upton thinks you should have a scallywag of your own."

My cousins all had *scallywags if their own* and were nauseatingly in love. It was fantastic for them even though they'd all chosen oddballs. Absurdly, they assumed I was next in the Mermaid Mating Game. I hated to disappoint them, but they were wrong—very wrong. I'd had my chance and it disappeared. I wasn't going there ever again.

"Don't want a scallywag," I informed my family. "Men are arses. Present company excluded," I said to Upton.

"While I mostly agree," Tallulah said with a sly smirk. "How long has it been since you've done the nasty?"

"Alrighty then," Upton yelled, turning pink in the face and getting seriously embarrassed. "Don't wanna hear the deets about me little Mermaid's quaffin' habits. Petunia's like me own wee bairn that I never had. Although, if me and the cackle fruit had a wee bairn, it'd be a little harrier than me Petunia. So, I'm gonna skeedaddle and work on me hygiene."

On that note, Upton sprinted out of the hut with his cookies in tow.

"He's gonna lick his nards," Ariel said with a giggle.

"Correct," I said as I swiped at a tear that rolled down my cheek.

I'd been secretly thinking of Upton as my weird little balding Pirate father since I'd met him. The fact that he was thinking the same overwhelmed me. Life was going good for a change. I just prayed to the diaper-wearing, drunk-assed Poseidon that it lasted.

"Back to my question. How long since you participated in the horizontal mambo?" Tallulah was all business—nosey business.

"A while," I admitted. While Mermaids were very sexual beings, I'd kind of lost my mojo.

"Define a while," Tallulah pressed.

"Twenty-five years," I whispered.

The hut went silent. My cousins exchanged alarmed and concerned glances.

Gods, it did sound awful when spoken aloud. It was all *his* fault. My runaway mate was the most spectacular nookie partner in the Universe. He'd ruined me for all others. His package alone was *insane*.

"A quarter of a century?" Tallulah gasped out.

"Yesssss," I hissed. "A quarter of a century."

Tallulah wouldn't understand. She was happily mated to the idiot and *very randy* Pirate Doug. The colossal mess of immortal idiocy also happened to be the son of Poseidon and heir to the throne. Gods help us all if Poseidon ever retired. Tallulah's Pirate-Vampire was the very same dimwit who had stolen her heart a century ago. He'd also pilfered all of my cousins' money because he was an asshat—although he did return it. The heart wanted what the heart wanted. Tallulah wanted Pirate Doug and got her wish. He was growing on me—like a non-contagious itchy rash.

"Immortal Snatch can solve your dry spell," Ariel said.

"Have you been snorting sand?" I asked with a laugh. "Anything called Immortal Snatch is not the way to meet a decent scallywag."

"Upton met Yolanda," she pointed out.

She was right. And while Upton and his cackle fish were bizarre, they were lovely. I hadn't even met Yolanda yet and I adored her.

"I just don't know," I said, grabbing a few cookies and inhaling them. Thank the gods that Mermaids had amazing metabolism. I'd eaten several dozen cookies over the last few days.

"It doesn't have to be a forever mate," Ariel insisted. "Just someone to have a little fun with. It's not normal for a Mermaid to be celibate."

It was if you'd been ruined for all others by the sexiest man alive. But that was info I wasn't going to share.

Ariel's mate Keith was a Selkie with the maturity level of a fourth-grade boy. However, the big dummy loved my blue-haired cousin to distraction and she loved his questionably intelligent ass right back. Misty's mate was a freakin' demigod—Cupid no less. He wasn't as dimwitted as Keith or Pirate Doug, but he came with his own set of challenges, which included an ego the size of the continental US.

And Madison? She'd found Rick—a vegan Werewolf with a death wish that matched hers. They'd just come back from blowhole diving in Hawaii. Madison and Rick had been instrumental in saving me from the Gnomes. As crazy as they were, I would fully support all of their lethal hobbies for eternity.

"Let's just look at some of the pictures," Misty suggested.

"Fine," I said, giving up. They weren't going to leave until I played the game. They wouldn't win, but I would play.

"How about him?" Tallulah asked, pointing to the screen. "He's a Merman."

"Nope, he's wearing a turtleneck alone. No jacket or sweater," I said, scrunching my nose. "Bad fashion sense."

"Agree," Ariel said with a nod. "Look at this one. He's a Warlock."

"He looks like a face eater," I said.

"A face eater?" Madison asked with a laugh.

I grinned and nodded. This was actually kind of fun. "Yep. Look at him. He looks like he'd try to eat your face when you made out."

"Sweet seashells on a Sunday, she's right," Misty said with a belly laugh. "Okay… what's wrong with this one?"

"Loud chewer," I replied with a giggle.

"Him?" Tallulah asked.

"Last name is Seamon. Not going there."

"She's good," Ariel said, getting into it with glee. "How about this one? He's a Werelion."

"That one looks like he has a foot fetish and would want me to put cheese between my toes so he could eat it," I explained.

My cousins were now on the floor of my hut rolling around in hysterics. It was the best day ever. Tallulah could barely breathe. It was lucky for her that Mermaids could hold their breath for a week at a time or she'd be a goner.

"One more," Ariel begged as she crawled over to the computer and scrolled for more pictures.

"Two more," Madison insisted as she pulled herself back together and joined Ariel.

"Two more and that's it. I have a freakin' sea monster to find and kill," I said, seating myself next to my cousins.

"Okay," Misty said, pointing to the screen. "Him?"

"Looks like he would have long toenails and bring me

flowers he stole from a cemetery," I said, feeling totally on my game as my cousins shrieked in laughter.

"Ohhhhhhhh," Tallulah said, gaping at the screen. "You won't be able to find anything wrong with this one. He's goooooorgeous. Take a peek at this hottie!"

And I did.

And I felt like I was going to faint.

There was no way in hell this could be happening.

The son-of-a-bitch left me high and dry twenty-five years ago and then joins a dating service called Immortal Snatch? What were the freakin' odds?

I felt dizzy and ill. There was no more laughter from my cousins. They'd seen me go from the quintessential Mermaid comedian to paler than a ghost. My body shook and it took all I had not to cry.

"You know him?" Tallulah whispered as she wrapped me in her arms and held tight.

Nodding, I decided I didn't have to hold back my tears. My girls loved me even with all my numerous faults and weaknesses. "He's the reason I haven't boinked anyone in a quarter of a century."

"Would you like us to kill him?" Madison asked, completely serious.

Giggling through my tears, I shook my head no. Never in my life had so many people had my back. "No. He just didn't want me. It's okay."

"It's not okay," Misty hissed. "It's bullshit. You're the catch of the freakin' century."

Misty had clearly been drinking seawater. I was no one's catch.

"Isn't that the Genie that streaked during the Super Bowl twenty-five years ago?" Ariel asked, squinting at the picture. "His salami was huge."

This was news to me. If he'd done something stupid like that, he'd done it after he'd disappeared from my life. I was busy swimming the Seven Seas after I'd gotten stood up on the day of my mating.

"It is him," Tallulah said, glaring at his face on the screen. "From what I recall, he also stole the Mona Lisa and went on TV to prove Genies exist. You're better off without a douchecanoe like that asshat."

None of those escapades sounded like the Delphinus I'd been in love with. They had to be mistaken—well, other than the enormous package. The rest was too out of character for the man I used to love. Whatever. It was a long time ago.

"Umm... guys," I said. "I'm gonna go for a swim and search for Charybdis. I'd really like to kill something right now. You feel me?"

"We do," Tallulah said, hugging me again. "I'll get Upton to go with you."

"Okay," I replied, needing the ocean to heal the old wounds that had come roaring back to the surface. The only thing that would make it perfect would be if the stars were out. "I'll be back in a few hours."

"Don't die," Ariel said. "If you do, we'll kill you."

"Roger that," I told her with a forced smile.

Right now death would be a relief. But before I died, I would kill the one who had killed my parents. Vengeance was my reason for survival right now.

"SHE STILL LOVES THE RAT BASTARD," TALLULAH SAID TO HER sisters.

"Yep," Ariel agreed. "It was written all over her face. I'd like to chop his impressive wanker right off his very handsome body and shove it down his throat."

"I'd like to twist that bastard into a pretzel and feed him to the sharks," Madison growled. "A man has to be right out of his debatably sane mind not to want someone as fabulous as Petunia. He's a complete bag of douche."

"You got that right," Misty hissed. "If I ever lay eyes on him, his Genie weenie is a goner. Petunia might not believe in herself, but I do. Sure, her exterior is gorgeous because all Mermaids are lookers, but her insides shine like the stars in the sky."

"She needs to believe that," Tallulah pointed out.

"We just have to keep loving her," Ariel said softly.

"That's easy," Madison told her sisters. "Petunia is completely lovable."

They thought I'd left, but I listened to their conversation through the open window of my hut as tears rolled down my cheeks. They were so wrong, but I wanted them to be so right. Was I lovable? I didn't feel it. Oh, I knew my parents loved me and I knew the girls did too. It was also clear that Upton adored me as I did him.

But me?

I didn't love me. And Delphinus didn't love me…

Well, screw him—not literally even though that would be pretty fabulous. I didn't need a man—didn't want one.

If my cousins and Upton thought I was lovable maybe I was.

It was time to go kill in the name of love. I'd just pretend that Charybdis was Del. It was fitting. I'd kill the old love so I could start brand new. Maybe I'd give a few of the weirdos on Immortal Snatch a try in a year or two from now.

Maybe.

I stayed a moment longer and eavesdropped a little more.

"Well, Pirate Doug's newly discovered brother is coming for a visit. Maybe he's not a douche and Petunia will like him," Tallulah announced. "We'll have a party and introduce them!"

"Umm… I'm gonna have to go with Pirate Doug's brother being a colossal douche," Ariel said with a giggle. "We can't unload an assmonkey on Petunia."

"She doesn't have to mate with him," Madison pointed out. "Just a no strings attached boink."

"Let's let Petunia pick her own douche," Misty suggested. "However, a party sounds like a great idea."

I would be sure to be *busy*. As much as I loved my cousins, I knew I wasn't ready to meet anyone. I needed to work on me first.

6
DELPHINUS

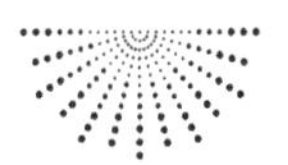

"RUN!" Pirate Doug bellowed as razor-sharp machetes whizzed past our heads. "The crayons with excellent knockers are trying to kill you… or me… or us. Just run for your farkin' life. The swimming hookers like to go for the nards."

"What the actual fuck?" I shouted as I sprinted across the beach and headed into the jungle area of the island.

"Up the palm tree," Doug screeched as he climbed like Hades was on the heels of his ridiculous knee-high boots.

I was no idiot. Doug most definitely was. I'd found that out in the first thirty seconds of speaking with my brother. However, the tree was a damned fine idea.

"Make no sound," he whispered as we balanced precariously two-hundred feet off the ground on a palm branch.

Below us, four furious Mermaids ran through the jungle wielding weapons and growling obscenities. At this point, I was pretty sure I wasn't going to make it till sundown. Pappy was an asshole.

"Doug, what the hell is going on?" I whispered, watching the violent women run farther into the jungle.

The dolt just stared at me. Was he deaf? I didn't think so, but I tried again facing him so he could read my lips if necessary.

"Doug," I said, over-annunciating and talking a little louder now that the posse from hell had passed. "What's up with the murderous Mermaids?"

My brother simply stared, crossed his arms over his chest and rolled his eyes. If I wasn't being hunted by four deadly Mermaids, I would have punched his face in. However, I needed the dumbass at the moment.

Doug huffed and puffed for three minutes. If we weren't in a tree, I was fairly sure the freak would have thrown a tantrum. Finally, after rolling his eyes so hard they should have gotten stuck in the back of his head, he decided to speak.

"Because our drunk off his arse Pappy said to be nice to you or he'll electrocute me, I will explain one more time. My name is *Pirate* Doug. The only one allowed to call me Doug is the purple-haired hellion leading the pack of vicious Mermaids. Tallulah's my mate."

"Your mate tries to kill you?" I asked, shocked. I mean, he was an imbecile but that wasn't a great reason for decapitation.

"Pretty sure they're trying to castrate you," Pirate Doug pointed out rather logically.

"Why? I've never seen any of them in my life."

"Did you ever abscond with their treasure?" my brother inquired with a raised brow.

"Of course not," I snapped. "That's an asshole move."

"Yes, well..." Pirate Doug stuttered, looking embarrassed. "I've been called worse, but that's not the point. Cleary, you did something to piss off the hookers Not real sure this is the right time for a visit for you if you value life."

Did I? Right now, I wasn't so sure. However, being decapitated by people I didn't know seemed like a bad way to die.

"Are there only four?" I asked. I'd seen one with blue hair, one with pink, one with green and one with purple hair—Pirate Doug's bloodthirsty mate, Tallulah. I was hoping to see an orange-haired beauty, but no such luck. Or maybe it was luck...

"Nay," Pirate Doug said. "There's more, but the ones you saw are related—sisters. Horrible vile women. You're gonna love them."

"Doubtful," I muttered, wondering if it was safe to get out of the tree. At this point, leaving the Mystical Isle seemed prudent. "Do you have any clue why they want to kill me?"

"Nope," he said. "Have you ever been around a Mermaid before?"

Nodding curtly, I kept the pathetic story to myself. I wasn't about to tell my dolt of a brother that I was basically left at the altar by the Mermaid love of my life.

"Do you know how to talk to the swimming hookers?" he asked.

"Umm…" Had that been my problem with Petunia? I hadn't thought so, but…

Pirate Doug eyed me for a long moment. "Fine, Delpenis. I'll teach you."

"Whoa, whoa, whoa," I said with a pained laugh. "It's Delphinus. Not Delpenis. Actually, just call me Del. That will save me having to kick your ass into the next century."

"My bad," he said. "Could have sworn Pappy called you Delpenis."

"He drinks. A lot," I pointed out.

"Correct," Pirate Doug said, his eyes narrowing with displeasure. "The diaper-wearing dingleberry called me Pirate *Slug*. Can you believe that shite?"

"Umm… no. That's awful," I said, trying not to smile. Doug was clearly hurt by the unflattering nickname. As ridiculous as the man was, I kind of liked him. I'd never had a brother before. Of course, I would have chosen someone who didn't wear skin-tight breeches and a puffy shirt, but beggars couldn't be choosers. And he did save my life.

"I'd like to grant you a wish for sparing me from castration by Mermaid, Pirate Doug," I told him.

My brother got so excited at the prospect of a wish that he squealed like a girl and fell out of the tree. I winced as I watched the idiot hit every branch on the way down. Coming here was a huge mistake. Why had I trusted Poseidon after one good smackdown? Maybe I was as stupid as my brother.

"I'm good," Pirate Doug yelled, hopping to his feet and popping his shoulder back into the socket. "Should I come back up or do you want to come down?"

"I'll come down," I told him as I snapped my fingers and my magic carpet appeared.

Floating down to the ground, I hopped off and stared at my *brother*. He was a hot mess—palm leaves were stuck in his breeches and his hair. Whatever. Not my problem.

"So, about that wish," Pirate Doug said, rubbing his hands together with glee. "Any ground rules?"

With an eye roll that beat his earlier one, I sighed. "You can't wish someone dead. I can't make anyone fall in love and I can't bring anyone back from the other side. Other than that, it's anything goes."

"First off, I'd like to congratulate you on your pecker," Pirate Doug said, slapping me on the back. "Biggest schlong I've ever seen on the Super Bowl."

"You've seen a lot of schlongs on the Super Bowl?" That confused him. Note to self—stay away from sarcasm with my *brother*. "Never mind. What is it that you want?"

"A bigger schlong, Delpenis," he announced, going for his pants to show me what he was working with at the moment.

"Do *not* pull down your pants, jackhole. And do not call me Delpenis. If you do, I'll call you Dong."

"It's Doug," he corrected me.

"I know," I snapped. "I was making a point."

He stared at me blankly.

Gods help me… "You see since you said Del*penis*, I gave you a dick name as well."

Still a blank stare.

"Dong," I said, trying to make him understand. "Dong is another term for dick. Get it?"

Pirate Idiot threw his head back and bellowed with laughter. "I like it," he yelled. "You can be Delpenis and I'll be Pirate Dong. The Immortal Universe will then know we're well-hung brothers."

How did that go so wrong? "Okay. No," I said flatly. "If you call me *Delpenis*, I'll remove your *dong*? You feel me?"

"Would it be a permanent removal?"

Was he serious?

He was.

"Yes, it will be permanent."

"Got it," Pirate Doug said as he went back to removing his breeches.

"STOP," I shouted. "I don't need to see your dong to make it larger. And if you pull it out, I'll kick your ass so hard it will come out of your mouth."

"Great," he said with a thumbs up. "Too many buttons on my fucking breeches anyway. Took me an hour to get them on this morning."

"Right," I said, thinking this was a very bad idea on his part. But I was just the Genie—the granter of wishes. Technically, I wasn't supposed to comment on what someone wanted. Right now, that was difficult.

"I want it about twice the size of yours," Pirate Doug announced. "Can't have a brother with a bigger salami than mine."

"You're joking," I said, trying not to laugh.

"Nay," Pirate Doug said. "Serious as a fart attack."

"You mean heart attack?" I asked, biting the inside of my cheek so I didn't laugh in his face. The dolt was actually growing on me. Although, my standards were a little low at the moment considering I'd been incarcerated in a bottle for twenty-five years.

"Nope. A fart attack. My man, Upton, made bean salad on our last pilfering voyage—deadly stuff. If I wasn't fucking immortal, I would have died from the smell of my own farts—very serious indeed, brother. And just a heads up, if Upton makes his salad for the party tonight, *do not* eat it."

"Are you always like this?" I asked. "Or is this a special occasion?"

"Not following," Pirate Doug said, looking perplexed.

"Of course, you're not," I said, shaking my head. Well, at least he was honest. "Can I give you a little brotherly advice?"

"Absolutely," he said.

"You might not want to go twice the size of my dick," I told him. "Might be kind of hard to walk, dude."

"Was that a pun?" Pirate Doug asked.

I had to think about it for a second and then I laughed. "It was a bad one, but yes."

"I knew it!" he said, dancing a little jig. "And don't you worry yourself about me walking. I'm the deadliest, best looking Vampire-Pirate on the High Fucking Seas. I'll be fine. I will be registering my wank in the Guinness Book of World Records later today."

His humility was nonexistent. This was a shitshow waiting to happen.

"Pirate Doug?"

"Yes, Delpenis?"

Ignoring the botched version of my name, I made one

last attempt to save my brother from himself. "I'm going on record and saying this is a very bad plan," I told him.

"Bad plan is my middle name," he assured me. "Let's do it!"

Well, I tried... With a wave of my hand, I gave my imbecile brother his wish. He immediately screamed and doubled over in pain since his tight breeches clearly racked him.

"New pair of breeches?" Pirate Doug wheezed, looking like he was going to pass out.

"That's two wishes."

"It's either that or I go schlong to the wind, brother," he squealed as his voice rose higher and higher.

"This one is a freebie," I said, snapping my fingers and giving him a pair of breeches that made room for his ample new appendage. He looked ridiculous since the crotch of his pants almost touched the ground, but he seemed delighted.

"Ahhhh," Pirate Enormous Package said in relief, as he waddled over to a large rock and tried to sit down.

He couldn't.

"Problem?" I asked with a grin.

"Might have made a little miscalculation on the size of my taco hammer," he said, trying desperately to find a position that didn't squash his new and improved manhood.

"You think?" I asked, with a shake of my head.

"Can we make it a little smaller but still bigger than yours?" he asked, still trying to find a position that wouldn't send him into agonizing pain.

I eyed my brother and wondered if the rest of the thousand siblings I had were as dimwitted as he was. Technically, it was his third wish, but he was blood-related. The binding didn't happen unless I granted three wishes to someone who was not in my family tree. Taking a deep breath, I said a prayer to every god I could think of that Pirate Dong wasn't illegitimate. Being bound to him for eternity was not my idea of a good time.

"Fine, I'll fix your dick. Then you have to hold up your end of the deal," I told him.

"Will do," he said. "And I'll throw in a case of rum that I stole from Pappy—good stuff."

With another wave of my hand, I fixed my brother's *dong* and gave him a new pair of breeches. His enormous sigh of relief made me laugh. Hopefully, he learned a lesson today, but somehow, I doubted it.

"YOU'RE *SURE* THEY LIKE TO BE CALLED SWIMMING HOOKERS?" I asked, taking a swig off the excellent bottle of rum.

Pirate Doug had snuck me out to his ship. He assured me that I was safe from the hookers here. Apparently, they refused to board his ship. I didn't blame them. It was a filthy shitshow of epic proportions.

"Aye," he said, nodding his head. "Swimming hooker is a term of endearment." He stopped mid-sip and gasped. "No. Wait. Don't call them swimming hookers. You'll get your bacon bazooka tied in a knot and your arse kicked out to sea."

Shaking my head, I groaned. What did I expect? My brother was an idiot.

"Always compliment their hooters with flowery language," he went on. "Variety is the rice of life."

"You mean spice," I corrected him.

"What?"

"Nothing."

"As I was saying," Pirate Doug continued with his horrifying suggestions. "I shake it up. For example, this morning I called Tallulah's bazongas *bone- inducing sweater puppets.*"

"How'd that go over?" I asked, closing my eyes and realizing I was going to die sooner if I used my brother's guidelines.

"Surprisingly well," he replied. "My purple-haired she-devil gut-punched me but didn't try to decapitate me. I call that a win. I almost went with shirt potatoes, but I'm saving that one for a special occasion."

"Let me know how that works out," I said.

"Will do, my brother," Pirate Doug replied and finished off the bottle.

He was no help at all. At least the rum was good. However, I still couldn't figure out how I was supposed to get my Genie Star Fire Light back here. Maybe Poseidon had sent me here to die quickly, instead of the slow agonizingly painful death that was coming for me. It was shitty, but somewhat compassionate in a soused kind of way.

"You could also kill our sister and earn some points with the hookers," Pirate Doug informed me.

"I'm sorry. What?" I asked certain I'd heard him wrong. "Kill our sister?"

"Aye," he replied. "Actually, Pappy disowned the scurvy

wench thousands of years ago. She's a murderous tar stain on the arse of society."

I held my tongue. As far as I could tell, his mate fit that description as well.

"How would that earn me points?" I asked, thinking my family was seriously fucked up.

"Charybdis is causing deadly whirlpools all around Mystical Isle. My Tallulah runs a tourist trap for humans and it's really screwing with business. Those whirlpools will suck even the strongest immortal to his death. Humans don't stand a chance. It's a black spot to the entire Immortal Universe."

My stomach clenched. My fingers began to spark and I set the deck of Pirate Doug's ship aflame. Quickly waving my hand, I put it out. The ship was filled with so much shit, it would go up like a rocket if the fire spread.

"Sorry," I muttered as I began to pace.

"No worries," he said. "Tallulah tries to blow up the ship weekly. It's our little game. Only sucks when I'm aboard."

Deciding to ignore my brother's difunctional relationship, I remembered my own. I could still remember the conversation like it was yesterday. I held my beautiful Petunia in my arms as she cried and told me of her parents' death. A deadly magical whirlpool had ended their lives. Thankfully, her father had thrown her to safety. The coincidence was too much to avoid.

"Is Charybdis the only being that can cause this kind of maelstrom?" I asked, feeling a fury consume me.

"Aye," my brother confirmed. "Only our sister, the murderous sea monster, is capable of creating a poisonous magical vortex like that. The wankin' hag has tried to scuttle my ship for centuries."

I now believed for sure that Poseidon had sent me to my death. However, I was fine with it. I couldn't have the Mermaid of my dreams, but I could avenge her and kill the one who had murdered her parents. Petunia might never know what I'd done for her, but I would. I'd die knowing I'd done right by her even though she didn't want me.

"I'll kill Charybdis," I said, standing up and feeling like I finally had a life purpose for what little life I had left. "The sea monster is mine."

"Ahhh shite. I forgot something," Pirate Doug said, bashing himself in the head with the rum bottle.

That had to hurt. "What?" I asked, wondering if he'd given himself a concussion.

"You might have to fight another vicious Mermaid," Pirate Doug said. "Someone else has called for the head of Charybdis. Although I'm sure the swimming hooker wouldn't mind a hand."

My heart began to beat rapidly in my chest. I felt light-headed and thought maybe Pappy hadn't sent me to my death after all. But there was only one way to find out…

"Who wants the head of Charybdis?"

"Petunia," Pirate Doug announced. "The cousin of my mate and every bit as insane. However, her mammary cannons are outstanding."

I wanted to punch his lights out for even noticing Petunia's ladybumps, but I reminded myself that she wasn't mine. Pirate Doug, as idiotic as he was, had my back. It was a bit terrifying, but it meant the world to me right now.

"Can you keep a secret, brother?" I asked him.

"You mean, like don't tell anyone?" he asked, trying to get it all straight.

"Yes. Like don't tell anyone. Can you do that for me?"

"You fixed and improved my disco stick," Pirate Doug said reverently. "Not to mention, you're my brother. I will keep your secret until the day I die."

So, I told him. I told him everything. Of course, I had to explain things two and three times before he actually understood. It was a relief to get it all off my chest. I needed an ally—a friend—a brother.

Pirate Doug stood up and offered me his hand. When I went to take it, the dumbass pulled me into an embrace and held me tight. It felt good. It felt right. It felt like this might be the beginning instead of the end.

"Delpenis and Pirate Dong forever," my brother shouted into the wind. "Two well-hung brothers who will WIN!"

And then again, I suppose it could be the end.

7
PETUNIA

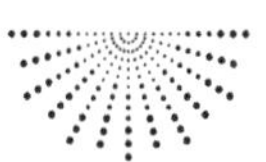

"THAT WAS FREAKIN' BIZARRE," I MUTTERED AS I WIGGLED MY nose and magically morphed my tail back to legs. Walking out of the salty sea, I turned and gazed out at the sparkling teal blue water. Squinting my eyes and staring at the waves, I told myself I was nuts. The ocean was usually my happy place, but not today.

The whirlpools were vicious and lethal and now multiplying. Charybdis was nowhere to be found. However, that didn't throw me off as much as the tricks my mind was playing on me.

"What was bizarre, lassie?" Upton asked, shaking the water off of himself like a dog after a bath.

"Did you hear two men talking while we were searching for Charybdis?"

"Aye, but methinks t'was only one scallywag blabberin'," Upton said with a nod. "Pirate Doug was on his ship most likely talkin' to himself. His brother is arriving later and we're havin' a shindig tonight to celebrate! Pirate Doug was probably practicing his speech so the wonderful swimmin' hooker, Tallulah, won't have to de-pecker him. Me Captain tends to say the wrong thing—if ye know what I mean." Upton giggled and then began to bounce on his toes. "I'm making me bean salad. Ye have to try it."

"I thought you couldn't cook," I said absently as I made my way back to my hut. I didn't even have the energy to correct Upton's insulting term for my kind. I felt wildly unsettled for some reason.

"Me bean salad is me one and only dish. A Pirate has to be able to concoct a hearty meal for his arses. I learned me bean salad from the cartoon channel," Upton said with pride.

"Well then, I'll definitely have some," I promised with a smile. Gods only knew what it would taste like since the cartoon channel wasn't really known for their recipes. "Umm… Upton?"

"Aye lassie?"

"I could have sworn on Poseidon's diaper I heard someone yell 'Delphinus and Pirate Doug forever. Two well-hung brothers who will WIN!' Did you hear that?" I asked, sure I was going insane.

"Nay, I heard 'Del*penis* and Pirate *Dong* forever. Two well-hung brothers who will WIN!"

"Oh," I said, feeling ridiculous. "That's an entirely different story. And seriously gross."

"Aye," he agreed. "Do ye want to help me make the bean salad? All ye have to do is open up thirty cans of beans and add mayonnaise and chocolate chips," Upton explained, clearly aware that I was off.

"Not today," I told him and kissed his bald head. Note to self—*do not* eat the bean salad. Ever. "Maybe another time."

"Don't ye worry yer pretty orange head, Petunia. We'll find Charybdis yet. The vile wench can't hide from us forever."

"Right," I said quickly. Of course, he thought my disquiet was due to coming up empty- handed again in our search for the murderous sea monster. He was wrong. But I didn't want to admit the real reason even to myself. It had to have been that I saw the jackhole's picture on Immortal Snatch. Now I thought I heard his dang voice. I needed a pina colada and a nice nap. "What time is the shindig?"

"Sunset on the beach," Upton said with a giggle. "And I've got a surprise for ye!"

"You didn't have to do that," I said somewhat terrified. As much as I adored Upton, he was still a nard licker and put chocolate chips in bean salad. Not sure a surprise was a good thing.

"Aye, tis nothin'," he said with a sweet smile. "I like to see ye happy."

My heart skipped a beat and I looked at my BFF slash pretend dad. He was a sopping mess and absolutely beautiful. His crooked little grin was perfect and his eyes twinkled like the stars I adored so much.

Taking his gnarled little hand in mine, I brought it to my cheek. "You make me very happy," I told him. "You're the best BFF I've ever had."

"Awww, ye make me blush like a cutlass flappin' scuttle hound, Petunia. Yar a good little lassie and I'm proud of ye."

I was taken aback. Why in the Seven Seas was Upton proud of *me?*

My BFF smiled and patted my head—kind of like I was a dog, but it was the thought that counted. It was as if he could read my mind. Maybe he could. He was a Sphinx after all.

"I'm proud that ye stayed here on the Mystical Isle and didn't run away. Ye is givin' life a real try. I'm proud that yar facing yar own monsters and letting the swimmin' hookers and me love ye."

His statement was so startling that I decided to completely overlook that he'd referred to my cousins—and ultimately me—as hookers. Was I really doing all that?

"And I believe ye've found a new callin'," Upton added.

"I have?"

"Ye have," he assured me with a wink. "Word around the Seven Seas is that ye've started a hitman service. Getting' rid of one stripey-sweatered sea monster at a time."

"Are you serious?" I asked, shocked.

"Nay. I'm Upton," he replied. "But I've been fieldin' a few calls for yer services."

I was almost speechless. "You have?" I whispered, realizing I maybe I had found my calling. I was really good at killing shit. I'd never thought about making it a business though. "How in the heck do people know?"

Upton blushed a bright pink and giggled nervously. "Well, I might have put yar new business on social media."

Okay, it was weird enough that Upton was on social

media, but the fact that he cared enough to think about me and help me find a job I wouldn't get fired from was amazing. Although, I was slightly concerned to find out what he'd posted.

"What did you say?" I asked cautiously.

"Well, umm... I named yer business and registered the trademark. Also incorporated ye and sent up yer business accounts at the last bank me and the arses robbed. Met some lovely people thar. Plus, they had excellent security installed after we cleaned 'em out. And while I was at it, I created ye a logo—a flame-haired Mermaid surrounded by stars, wieldin' a huge machete. I put yer logo and me cell phone number on social media and my phone has been ringing off the hook!"

"Wow," was all I could say. My BFF had been busy. However, there was still one thing I needed to know. "What exactly did you *call* my new business?"

I held my breath and waited. After I'd learned what Poseidon had named his dating service Immortal Snatch, I was wary. Upton did enjoy becoming one with his nards.

Although, my little buddy had done so much for me that I was going to stick with whatever he named my new career venture—no matter how horrifying. To think that Upton had figured out the one thing I was good at and turned it into something lucrative was mind-blowing. My limber BFF humbled me.

"If ye don't like it, ye can change it," Upton said quickly. "Won't hurt me feelings a bit, lassie."

"Tell me," I said with a laugh. I mean, how bad could it be?

Upton took a deep breath, puffed his chest out and slowly slid into a left side split. "Arsehole Assassinations compliments of Petunia the Sea Monster Slayer!" he crowed with delight.

It was horribly fantastic—and very long. I would have chosen something vastly different, but I never would have come up with the idea in the first place.

"I love it," I said, trying to slide into the splits alongside him, but only getting halfway there. "And I love you."

"I love ye too, little Mermaid," Upton said as he helped me untangle myself from my awkward position. "And just so ye know, it was all me cackle fruit's idea."

"Yolanda hatched this plan?"

"Aye," he said. "All except for the name of yer new business. That was all me!"

"You did great," I assured Upton, hugging the little man. "Do my cousins know?"

"Aye," he said, doing a fancy little jig that reminded me of someone having to go to the bathroom really bad. "Tallulah had t-shirts and hats made up with yer logo on 'em. And the violent lovely lassies created an office space for ye in the lodge—even made a little area for me since I'll be yer handler. The thoughtful swimmin' hookers also put a door on me space so I could have privacy to cleanse me gangoolies! Me cackle fruit t'will be so delighted that ye like the plan."

"I can't wait to meet Yolanda and hug her too."

"Might come sooner than ye think. Mebbe *really soon*," Upton said with a secretive smile, rocking back on his heels and trying to hide his excitement.

Well, crap. I'd bet my orange tail that my surprise was Yolanda's arrival. Tonight. I'd had no intention of going to the shindig, but I wouldn't disappoint Upton for anything in the world.

"I'll see you at sundown," I promised my giggling BFF.

"Don't be late, lassie! Life is lookin' up!"

Life certainly was looking *up*. And *Up*ton was a big reason for that.

I'd already met my pretend dad. Tonight, I would meet my pretend mom.

I couldn't wait.

"YOU *HAVE* TO WEAR SOMETHING SEXY TONIGHT," MISTY insisted, going through my bikini tops and sarong skirts like her life or mine depended on it. "You need to rub it in major."

"Umm... pretty much all my clothes are sexy," I said, perplexed. Rub what in?

My four cousins paced my hut in distress with odd expressions on their lovely faces. Not to mention, they were all scratched up and Ariel had palm leaves in her blue hair. I was fairly sure it wasn't a fashion choice since they were placed haphazardly. While the scrapes on their arms and legs were healing quickly, the looks on their faces were positively strange.

Wait. A. Minute.

They knew about my surprise.

"Oh my gosh," I said with a laugh as I shook my head and

realized how much my cousins truly loved me. "I get it. I know who's going to be at the shindig. I think it's sweet that you want me to look nice."

"Sweet?" Tallulah asked, wildly confused.

"Yep," I assured her with a smile. "Upton let it out of the bag. I'm excited."

Misty's knees gave out and she dropped to the couch. "Excited?" she whispered in shock.

Did they not like Yolanda? If they didn't, I would definitely set their asses straight. If Upton loved Yolanda, all of us were going to love her. Period. Maybe they'd never met a Yeti. I certainly hadn't and I couldn't wait.

"You know who's here?" Ariel asked, paling considerably.

They were starting to piss me off. I never thought my cousins were speciests. Hating a species because they were hairy, liked to lead humans on wild goose chases and loved cookies was all kinds of wrong. What the heck was going on here? I watched as they exchanged furtive glances with each other and I wanted to smackdown on all of them. This was unacceptable. Upton would be devastated if he could hear them being so awful about his beloved cackle fruit.

"Of course I know," I ground out. "And I'm happy about it."

"You are?" Madison asked as her eyes went wide.

Enough was enough.

"Yesssssss," I snapped. "When Upton told me, I was thrilled. I can't wait. Although, I really think looking too sexy might be kind of weird. I want to make a good impression."

"I am so confused," Ariel muttered.

"So, we're not supposed to kill it?" Tallulah choked out.

"Have you been smoking seaweed?" I shouted. "First of all, it's not an it. It's a person with feelings. I can't believe you would kill an important guest that comes in peace. What has gotten into you girls?"

"I don't know. We thought we were doing you a favor," Ariel said, looking like she wanted to cry. "We almost succeeded in decapitation earlier today. Now I'm so glad we failed."

"Sweet shit on a seashell," I yelled as my hair began to blow around my head and my fingers shot sparkling orange flames. "Are you hookers trying to ruin my life? I've waited so long for this day to come. I mean, I know it's pretend, but it means the world to me. If you kill my surprise, I can't have a family."

"You want to have a family with it?" Misty asked with a flabbergasted look on her face as she pulled on her green hair.

"It's not an IT," I shouted and zapped all four of my cousins at the same time. I was that good. Being an assassin was going to work for me. "Sorry, guys."

"It's fine," Tallulah said, snapping her fingers and dousing the flames. "We had no clue you felt this way. We're really sorry."

"Do you promise to be nice?" I asked.

"We do," Madison promised. "In fact, we'll go apologize now."

"We'll make it right," Ariel added. "We'll do anything for you, Petunia. You have to know that."

"We'll even grovel," Misty said.

I sighed and looked at my cousins. Maybe something bad had happened with a Yeti in their past. In my heart, I knew Yolanda was a beautiful person. Upton wouldn't love her so much if she was evil. Maybe once they sat down and got to know her everything would be fine. In fact, I knew it would. My cousins were truly good people. This was just a horrible misunderstanding. As long as Yolanda hadn't been decapitated, it would all work out.

"Thank you," I said. "That means the world to me."

"Alrighty then," Tallulah said, moving toward the door of my hut. "We'll see you at sundown?"

"You will," I told the girls as they filed out still looking a bit perplexed.

I'd done a good thing today. I was beginning to like myself… maybe even love myself a little. Teaching my family that all species were made equally important was a fine start.

Except for sea monsters. They were assholes.

After tonight, I would find Charybdis and eliminate her. I had a new business and a reputation to uphold. If I was going to be an assassin, I was going to be a kickass one.

8
DELPHINUS

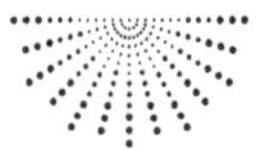

It wasn't my finest moment. When I opened my eyes from my nap on the piece of shit lawn chair that my brother had informed me he'd pilfered from Target, I screamed—like a girl. I screamed like a fucking girl.

In my defense, they were all standing over me and were within castration distance.

"Dude," the purple-haired one said—who I was pretty sure was Tallulah, my brother's mate. Which of course meant there was something seriously wrong with her. "Ease up. We come in peace."

"Your over-sized disco stick is safe," the pink-haired one said with a friendly smile.

Great, they'd seen the Super Bowl too. Apparently, I would never live that moment of insanity down. Since I'd been released from the pokey, I had yet to meet someone who hadn't seen my junk.

This had to be a trick. If I killed them, my brother would

probably be pissed. He seemed to like the hellcats. However, if I did nothing, I'd probably die a violent death. Shit. The choices were not good.

"Is this a boobytrap?" I asked in a lower tone than I usually used. I had to make up for screaming like a girl.

"Boobytrap is partyboob spelled backwards," my traitorous asshole of a brother announced, joining my death posse. The crazy Pirate was grinning like a fool and gave me a thumbs up.

I had to think for a minute to figure out if the idiot was correct. He was.

Eyeing the vicious murdering Mermaids, I weighed my options. Had Pirate Doug given me *any* accurate information on how to communicate with seafaring executioners? Only one way to find out. I was dying anyway. What did it matter? A swift death by a foursome with nice racks wouldn't be the worst way to go. However, these Mermaids didn't hold a candle to my Mermaid—who wasn't exactly mine.

"Good afternoon, swimming hookers," I said as pleasantly as I could without wincing at the words leaving my lips. "Your… umm… hooters are looking exceptionally perky and bodacious today. I've haven't seen such umm… nice shirt potatoes in quite a while."

"She likes him?" the green-haired one said with an eye roll. "Seriously?"

I needed to do better. Clearly, I hadn't impressed the homicidal maniacs with my first attempt.

"Lovely day," I went on, racking my brain for offensive terms for knockers. From what Pirate Doug had shared, the worse the nickname the better. "My drunk-assed pappy, Poseidon, didn't tell me what enormous lady nuts you gals had. If I'd known about the blouse balloons you were sporting, I would have visited my imbecile brother sooner. Your sweater stretchers put all other chest pillows to shame."

They were either appalled or impressed. All four Mermaids stood silently with their mouths hanging open. Pirate Asshole gave me a wink so I kept going.

"Yabos like yours are rare. From here it appears that your jigglejogglers are real, which is quite impressive. Fun bubbles like the ones protruding from your chests are my reason for living. For a while I considered changing my name to Chesticles Melons. However, since Genies are named after the star they represent and no star is named Chesticles Melons I was unable to change my moniker. However, I'm planning on talking to whoever is in charge about naming a few stars after mammaries in your honor."

"Is he right in the head?" the one with blue hair whispered, looking at me like I was a fungus growing science experiment.

Which was exactly what I felt like after uttering all the ludicrous bullshit. However, I was still alive, so maybe Pirate Doug had been correct.

"Doug," Tallulah hissed, turning and smacking her mate in the head. "Did you teach your brother how to talk to a Mermaid?"

"Maybe," Pirate Doug said, ducking an outstanding left hook from his mate. "But he came up with some stuff just now that I need to put on my knockers list. My brother is brilliant."

"Your brother is a bigger dumbass than you are," Tallulah informed him, giving me the stink eye. "However, we're here to apologize for trying to lop his wanker off with a machete earlier today."

"You are?" I asked, cautiously moving a safe distance away from the crazed posse.

"We are," the green-haired killer said. "It was a misunderstanding."

"That was quite a misunderstanding," I muttered, keeping my hands over my jewels.

"It happens. And we are so happy we didn't kill you," the blue one said. "It would have been just awful."

Pirate Doug, who was now hiding behind a barrel to avoid further maiming from his mate chimed in. "He's dying anyway. Might be kinder to behead my brother with the monster package. Although, mine is bigger," he added with a bow.

"Dude," I snapped. "What part of *can you keep a secret* didn't you understand?"

"Shite, my bad. Sorry, Delpenis," he shouted and then banged his head on the barrel so hard he passed out.

Thankfully, he was immortal and would wake up eventually. As stupid as he was, he was my brother and my only ally on this dangerous isle.

"Your name is Del*penis*?" Tallulah asked with a sour look on her face.

"No. No my name is not Del*penis*. It's Delphinus. I go by Del. My brother's an ass and can't get my name right," I said, ready to call to my magic carpet if the meeting went any farther south than it already had. "And I'd like to apologize for my disgusting dialogue. Doug said you gals love talk like that."

"He lets you call him Doug?" Tallulah asked, surprised.

"Actually, no," I admitted. "But since he's down for the count, I figured I could call him whatever I want."

"P.S. We hate the boob speak and don't ever call us swimming hookers or we'll call you Delpenis," Tallulah added.

"Got it," I said with a small smile. At least I had some legit ground rules now.

"I like to call Pirate Doug a gaping douchecanoe of utter stupidity," the one with blue hair volunteered with a giggle. "Oh, and I'm Ariel. We're really sorry that we tried to kill you."

"Okay," I said, still not trusting that they were sincere. "Thank you. And I'm glad I didn't kill you when I woke up. I think."

"I'm Madison," the pink-haired one said with slightly narrowed eyes.

She didn't trust me. That was fine. I didn't trust any of them.

"I'm Misty," the green-haired Mermaid told me. "You're dying?"

She certainly got to the point.

Nodding, I decided not to go into the particulars. It was none of their business. Besides, it was embarrassing. Petunia was their cousin.

"That's not good," Tallulah said, eyeing me with concern. "She'll be devastated."

"Who will be devastated?" I asked, as my stomach turned a flip flop.

"Petunia," Madison said. "She wants to start a family with you. I don't think you deserve her, but she loves you apparently."

"Are you sure you have the right Genie?" I asked as my heart pounded wildly in my chest.

"Sadly, yes," Misty said, glaring at me. "After what you did, I don't know why she still loves you."

Shit. Was the nude run at the Super Bowl going to follow me until I died? I could fix this. I had to fix this. If Petunia really loved me, we could start over. Occasionally the truth could set you free. I hoped this was one of those times.

"I was completely and utterly drunk," I volunteered quickly. "I can't be held responsible for my actions. I regret it completely and would do anything in the Universe to take it back."

The Mermaids exchanged glances and Tallulah stepped forward.

"So, you'll never run like that again?" she asked.

"Absolutely not," I replied, crossing my heart to show my sincerity. Showing my pecker to the world was idiocy personified. "By far the stupidest thing I ever did."

"Fine," she said with her purple eyes sparking ominously. "But if you ever hurt her like that again, your Gennie weenie is toast. You feel me?"

"I do," I said with a wide grin and a delighted laugh, feeling the happiest I had in twenty-five years. "Petunia really wants me?"

"Yep," Tallulah said. "I think she's insane, but then again I mated with Pirate Passed Out over there. Mermaids are idiots when it comes to love."

"That's fantastic," I shouted. "Fucking fantastic."

"We'll see," Madison said, still eyeing me warily.

She could eye me however she wanted. Life was fanfuckingtastic. Whatever I'd done to make Petunia leave the first time, I would never do again.

This time I was going to get it right.

The longevity of my dick and my happiness depended on it... not to mention my life.

"If you really want to get into your Mermaid's thong, I'd suggest borrowing one of my spiffy outfits for the shindig," Pirate Doug proposed, going through his closet in his cramped and messy quarters.

The Mermaids had high-tailed it back to the island several hours ago and my brother had come to a good while after their departure. I'd been left alone with my thoughts for a bit. I was like a human kid on Christmas morning. I paced like a madman. Unsure of what to do with myself, I began to clean my brother's shitty ship. I hadn't made it below yet, hence his room was still a shitshow.

"I look fine," I said, glancing down at my black t-shirt, black pants and combat boots. It was my bad-assed Genie look. Petunia had always loved it.

"I thought Genies went shirtless and wore puffy pants and a head wrap with jewels," my brother said, holding up an enormous pile of lace that I think was supposed to be a shirt.

"Some do," I said, refusing to even touch the horrifying piece of material that he held out to me. "I'm not your typical Genie."

"Nay, you're not," he said with a laugh. "Pappy said you kicked his ass. Would have loved to have seen that. With all due respect—which means none—that soused jackhole deserves a smackdown."

I grinned. "It was liberating—excellent to fight someone without worrying about killing them. The drunk bastard's head is as hard a rock. A solid freakin' punch to the head is exhilarating."

"That's the way I feel about my singing," Pirate Doug announced proudly. "I can kill anyone dead where they stand after only a few bars."

"I'm sorry. What?" I asked, squinting at him. I was well aware that my brother was confused about... well, almost everything. Did he really think he could destroy an enemy by singing?

"Yep," he went on proudly. "Blew up a fuck-ton of Krakens with my warbling."

"For real?" If he was telling the truth, that was jaw-dropping.

"One hundred percent." Pirate Doug nodded and tried again to hand me the lacy frock.

"I'm impressed," I told him, pretending I didn't notice the disaster in his hands. "You know if Petunia mates with me, I won't die."

Doug's eyes grew wide. "Is that a secret too?"

Shit. Why was I telling the imbecile things I shouldn't? Maybe reverse psychology would work here… Doubtful, but worth a shot.

"Umm… no. Not a secret," I said carefully, wondering about the wisdom of my new ploy. Doug *aka Dong* was definitely not a mental gymnast so I was hoping this plan of action would work.

I didn't want Petunia to feel like she *had* to mate with me to save my life. That would be far worse than death. Petunia had to want me for me. I was aware I wasn't a prize, especially after my famous Super Bowl run, but I'd done my time in the bottle

"Maybe I'll wear some puffy pants and a jeweled headpiece in honor of you, my brother," Pirate Doug said, searching through his closet. "I'm sure I have a costume in here. Tallulah likes to get spicy and I ordered a bunch of shit to turn her hot purple ass on."

"Her ass is purple?" I asked even though I really didn't want the answer.

"Nay. It's a finger of speech."

"You mean *figure*," I corrected him.

"You got that right, my man," Pirate Doug said with a hearty laugh. "My swimmin' hooker's figure is outstanding."

It was time for a change of subject. One of the more alarming qualities of my brother—and there were many—was that he was distracted as easily as a five-year-old.

"So, tell me more about Charybdis," I said, realizing if I did away with the sea monster, I would earn points with both Petunia and her crazy cousins.

"No one knows much," Pirate Doug said. "The vermin is sneaky and likes to hide."

"Could you kill her with a song?" I asked, curious.

"Probably," he said. "But I'd most likely blow out the eardrums of everyone within a three- hundred-mile radius. It would be seriously bad for my swimmin' hooker's business."

"Got it," I said, wondering if he had been dropped on his head as a baby. "Not to worry. I plan to kill the shit out of it."

"You know," my brother said, scratching his head. "I always heard Genies weren't good fighters."

"Normally they're not. Or at least not the male Genies. The females are foul-mouthed savages," I told him.

"Aye," Pirate said with a shudder and a grin. "Kind of like the swimmin' hookers."

"Kind of," I agreed with a chuckle. "However, I'm not just a Genie."

Pirate Doug's smile widened as he slowly figured out what I meant. It took him five minutes and twenty seconds. I waited patiently for the idiot's brain to work.

"That's right!" he bellowed as he stripped and put on a Genie costume that was so horribly insulting I almost punched him in the head. "Delpenis and Pirate Dong forever! Two well-hung brothers who also happen to be mother humpin' gods!"

I laughed. There was no way I couldn't. And he was actually correct—humility-free, but correct.

Life was looking up. Finally.

9
PETUNIA

"WHERE IS SHE?" I ASKED, SPRINTING ACROSS THE SAND TO Upton.

My mass of orange curls bounced around my head in the fragrant evening ocean breeze. I'd let it go wild and free since I figured my pretend mom would be pretty hairy. I'd chosen a teal jeweled bikini top and a teal and orange sarong. My feet were bare, but I'd painted my toenails teal too. I wanted to be put together and looking my best for the new Yeti in my life.

I hadn't felt this excited in twenty-five years. The last time I felt this kind of joy was when my pathetic joke of a mating that didn't happen because the turd-knocking asshead didn't want me. Tonight wouldn't end in heartbreak. I was sure of it.

My BFF was busy putting the worst looking bean concoction I'd ever seen onto the loaded down buffet table.

My cousins had outdone themselves for Yolanda. The beach looked like a magical island paradise. Tiki torches blazed and twinkling white lights lit the palm trees that surrounded the secluded area my cousins used for their shindigs. Not a human was present at this immortal party—just family and close friends. It was perfect.

I sighed with happiness. My girls were doing their best to make up for trying to kill Upton's and my cackle fruit. It warmed my heart and made me love them even more than I already did. I knew once they met her and got over their fear of Yetis that everything would be awesome.

Glancing around, I tried to spot my pretend mom. I wondered if Yolanda was always in Yeti form or if she had a human-looking form like other shifters. Whatever. Furry or not, I was already in love. I could only hope she was as excited to meet me as I was to meet her.

Sparkling seashell centerpieces sat atop the festively decorated tables. And the food? The food smelled wonderful. Well, except for Upton's bean salad—which smelled like something that had been pulled out of the garbage after a week… in August.

"Would ye like to try it?" Upton asked, spooning me up an enormous bowl.

"Umm… what's in it again?" I asked, trying to keep the bile in my stomach instead of my mouth.

"Beans, mayo, chocolate chips and I added some hard-boiled eggs and Limburger cheese to fancy it up," he replied with the pride of someone who had no business in a kitchen. Ever. "Watch out for the eggshells. Methinks I peeled 'em right, but them little bow bunglers are slippery!"

"I'll have some later," I promised with my fingers crossed behind my back. "Where's Yolanda? She's the reason I'm here."

"Yolanda comes tomorrow, lassie," Upton said, taking a taste of his culinary creation and spitting it onto the ground. "Don't eat the bean salad. Methinks the eggs might be rancid."

"Okay," I said, feeling deflated and wanting to cry. "But I thought you said she was my surprise for tonight."

"Nay, lassie. Sorry if ye misunderstood. Tis me own fault," Upton said, giving me a sweet hug. "Yolanda is so excited to meet ye that she had her beard braided and dyed orange to match yer hair! Me cackle fruit is giving the humans one last good chase before me scurvy wench takes a vacation."

I was confused. If Yolanda wasn't here, that meant my cousins hadn't tried to decapitate her. Of course, it also meant they weren't speciests—which was terrific. However, I couldn't for the immortal life of me figure out who they'd tried to kill in my honor.

Not to mention, I was a little thrown that my pretend mom had a beard. Whatever. I was cool with that. It was sweet that she'd dyed it orange. But if it wasn't Yolanda, who in the heck had my cousins tried to exterminate?

Shit on a flaming seashell. Was it Charybdis? Had I mistakenly led them to believe that I was cool with the sea monster that had killed my parents? It definitely made sense of their earlier strange reactions in my hut. Had Upton made bean salad for a sea monster?

Wait. Maybe the bean salad would kill the sea monster…

"Upton," I said as my pulse raced and my fingers began to spark. "Who is this shindig for?"

"It's fer Pirate Doug's brother," he replied, still gagging from taking a taste of his dish. "Haven't met the bloke yet, but the swimmin' hookers have rolled out the red carpet on account of ye."

"Of me?" I asked, not following at all.

"Aye," Upton said with a wink. "Word is that ye want to start a family with the dingy dangler. I'm real proud of ye, Petunia. Givin' the greasy-haired sea rat a second chance is a right fine notion. Me and me cackle fruit would love to have some grand-wee-bairns to teach how to pilfer. But if the cutlass flappin' fish stink treats ye wrong this time, it's a trip to Davy Jones' locker for the scallywag."

What in the flaming seashells was my BFF talking about?

"He's here and he's hot!" Ariel squealed as she ran up to me and hopped up and down in the sand. "At first, I thought he was brain damaged like Pirate Doug, but he's not."

"That's nice," I said, plastering a fake smile on my lips as my stomach roiled. Clearly, I had accidentally led my cousins to believe I was going to boink Pirate Doug's brother. I didn't even know Pirate Doug's brother. And there was no way the Seven Seas I was going to boink anyone who was related to Pirate Doug.

"After we set him straight that waxing disgustingly poetic about our knockers was bad form, he seemed okay," Madison said, joining Ariel and giving me a hug.

"We are soooo relieved we didn't de-wank or behead him," Tallulah said, taking my hand and squeezing it. "We would have felt just horrid if we had."

"Right," I said, trying to figure out how I was going to get out of this.

"And if his junk is as big as it looked on TV, you're gonna have a GREAT night," Misty said with a wide grin.

"Pirate Doug's brother is a porn star?" I whispered in shock and disgust. How much more horrifying could this get?

"Not as far as we know," Tallulah said. "I mean, he probably could be with that Johnson, but he doesn't seem the type."

"You've all seen his Johnson?" I choked out.

What was wrong with this dude? Had he shown up and waved his Johnson around? Was that why they'd tried to castrate him? Pressing my fingers to the bridge of my nose, I tried not to laugh or scream. This was a mess.

"I'd bet our treasure chest that most of the world has seen his Johnson," Ariel said, completely serious. "And just so you know, he apologized—said he was completely drunk."

"When he showed the world his Johnson?" I asked, trying to piece the alarming story together.

"Well, probably," Tallulah said. "Poseidon is his father. Getting soused and doing stupid shit runs in the family. But, no. He apologized for not showing up to your mating because he was wasted."

Oh. My. Gods.

No. Freakin'. Way.

My hair began to blow around my head and my fingers shot out sparkling streams of orange flame. The buffet table was now on fire. This was not necessarily a bad thing since it meant no one would get food poisoning from Upton's bean salad.

"Petunia?" Tallulah said in alarm. "You okay?"

"Nope," I snapped as I waved my hands in a circular motion. The gentle ocean breeze picked up and blew all the seashell centerpieces right off of the festively decorated tables. "Where is he?"

"Over there," Ariel whispered in fear as she pointed to the left.

My head whipped to the direction she'd pointed and my stomach dropped to my toes. There he stood, looking every bit as beautiful as I remembered him—six foot four of blond-haired, perfectly muscled perfection. His lashes were stupidly long and his lips were so kissable, it made me dizzy.

Delphinus—the rat bastard—stood next to his brother, Pirate Doug. The Pirate looked ridiculous clad in some kind of dime-store Genie costume. Del was in head to toe black. I was in such a state of shock, I couldn't decide if I wanted to zap the shit out of him or tackle him and play tonsil hockey.

"What is *he* doing here?" I growled at my cousins.

"Shit," Tallulah muttered. "We should have killed him."

"No worries," I said, as I walked slowly across the sand. "I can do it."

The guests ducked and ran for cover. The smile that had been on Delphinus' absurdly pretty face only moments ago disappeared. Pirate Doug tried to pull his brother to safety, but the idiot Genie was having none of it. He stood his ground and waited for me to kick his ass.

That was weird. Why wasn't he afraid?

"Why are you here?" I demanded, hoping my expression looked pissed because my insides were tingling wildly with desire.

I was not stupid.

I would not jump him.

I would not kiss him.

And I certainly wouldn't boink him.

"I love you," he said warily. "I'm sorry for displaying my junk during halftime of the Super Bowl twenty-five years ago."

Well, that certainly explained why everyone had seen his pecker. However, that wasn't the issue at the moment.

"If you love me why didn't you show up?" I snapped, narrowing my eyes and getting ready to zap his bitable ass.

The look of confusion on his face would have been amusing if he hadn't ruined my life.

"What are you talking about?" Delphinus asked, squinting at me in disbelief. "*You* didn't show up."

The oohs and ahhs from the dummies hiding under the tables sounded like the background music of a seriously bad B movie.

"Good one," I hissed, flicking my fingers and sending an orange flame of magic that set his shirt on fire.

Removing his flaming shirt much to the pleasure of all the women present, he glared at me like I was insane.

"You have some nerve, Petunia," Del growled. "After you stood me up, I went nuts."

"That's when Delpenis got soused and unveiled his

impressive beef bullet at the Super Bowl," Pirate Doug shouted from the top of a palm tree.

"My name is not Delpenis, you imbecile," Del shouted at his brother.

"My bad," Pirate Doug yelled back.

"I can't believe this shit," I muttered as I grabbed a seashell chair and dropped onto it while still glaring at the lying sack of sand staring at me. "You are so full of it."

"You're one to talk," Del shot right back. "You said you loved me and then bailed."

The oohs and ahhs were louder now and more emotional if I wasn't mistaken. I was about to zap everyone's ass here.

"I cannot believe you can stand there and lie like that," I said, feeling like I was going to cry. "And even if that were true, WHICH IT'S NOT, why didn't you try to find me?"

Delphinus went silent. His chin dropped to his chest and my heart shattered to a million pieces… again. So much for an evening without heartbreak.

"My brother with the grand mandingo was put into the glass pokey for twenty-five years," Pirate Doug shouted as he fell out of the tree and landed with a thud in the sand next to his brother. "Showing your pork sword on national television is apparently against the law. I didn't know this, but it's true. Call me crazy…"

"Crazy," Del said with an eye roll aimed at his brother. "You are batshit crazy."

"Thank you," Pirate Doug replied sincerely and continued. "As I was saying, my brother with the massive zipper sausage was incarcerated by a bunch of girly-pants-wearing Genie bastards who were jealous and threatened by his outstanding trouser snake. However, I'd like to announce that due to a wish granted by my large knobbed brother, my peepee is now slightly bigger than his."

The crowd went silent. No oohs and ahhs for the idiot Pirate.

"Is that true?" Tallulah choked out from under a table.

"Yes," Pirate Doug shouted triumphantly to his mate and then continued to overshare. "My first choice of a new dong size was a disastrous mistake. Couldn't sit down without racking the shit out of myself. Delpenis was very kind to fix my miscalculation. I have a wonderful and loving brother."

"TMI, dude," Delphinus said to his brother. "You should stop talking. Now."

"Right," Pirate Doug said.

Delphinus stared at me for a long moment. My instinct was to run into his strong arms and hold him tight. His eyes looked so dull and sad. He'd lost his sparkle.

"It's okay that you didn't show up," he said in a gentle voice that rolled over me like a warm ocean wave. "I don't blame you. I'm no prize."

"I'm no prize," I countered.

"Yes, ye are a prize," Upton bellowed from somewhere in the bushes. "And good news! The bean salad made it through the fire!"

"I thought I smelled that horrible shite," Pirate Doug muttered. "No one eat the bean salad. You'll die from a fart attack or possibly a shart attack."

"Everyone shut your cakeholes," I shouted. "You're not helping."

The crowd thankfully stayed silent.

"As I was saying," I went on looking at the Genie who used to be my world. "I'm no prize, so I don't blame you for running while you could."

"But I didn't," Delphinus insisted. "I was there."

Tears rolled down my cheeks. Had he spent so much time in the pokey that he'd rewritten history? Did he feel so badly about what he'd done, he'd turned it all around in his head?

"It's okay," I whispered and gave him a small smile. "It's the past and that's where it should stay. I wish you the best, Delphinus. I really mean that."

"My best is only with you," he said. "It always was."

"Can I say something here?" Pirate Doug asked with his hand raised high.

"Will it include a description of my junk?" Del asked with a loud sigh.

"Umm... no, but it can."

"NO," everyone yelled from their hiding places.

Pirate Doug laughed and began to impart his wisdom or lack thereof. "As I see it, this sounds like a whole lot of misunderstanding," Pirate Doug said sounding logical for the first time in his life. "It's apparent that both of you still have intense feelings for each other and have been pining away. Neither one of you is happy without the other. So, I say forget the past. Does it really matter who's right and who's wrong? Every single person here could die of a shart attack later tonight if they eat Upton's bean salad. Life—

even for immortals—is not guaranteed. If Tallulah had any sense in her head, she wouldn't love someone like me—even though I have an outstanding bacon bazooka. So, what do you say? Maybe go on over to Petunia's hut and play a little hide the salami and start living life again."

"You are so getting laid tonight," Tallulah called out to her mate. "Some of that was actually poetic."

"The part about my bacon bazooka?" Pirate Doug asked, quite pleased with himself.

"No, not that part," she replied with a laugh.

I glanced up at Delphinus. He was staring at me with so much love in his sad eyes that I nodded my head. His smile lit his face, but the light in his eyes was still dull. Something jerked in my stomach—a fear—an irrational fear.

Maybe Pirate Overshare was right. The past was the past. The future could be what we made of it. Did it matter that Del thought I didn't show up? Kind of. But with time and newly found trust maybe we could work through it. Or maybe it didn't matter. Timing was everything.

Maybe we'd had the timing wrong twenty-five years ago. Maybe now, the time was right.

Holding out my hand to the Genie who had haunted my dreams for a quarter of a century, I smiled.

"Come back to my hut. Let's talk," I said.

"Is that code for getting into the bone zone?" Pirate Doug asked.

Delphinus turned and punched his brother in the face. Pirate Doug went flying and then got up and laughed like a loon.

"It is not code for anything," Del told his brother. "It's

what I've dreamed of for twenty-five years. Just seeing Petunia's smile is making all my dreams come true."

Delphinus was a charmer—but then again most Genies were.

I prayed to every god I could think of that we could really give it a second try.

10
DELPHINUS

Petunia's very swanky hut was surprisingly clean. I'd recalled her being messy. But then I also recalled showing up to our mating... We were both nervous. I had a lot riding on this, but that was my secret. If she didn't want to try again that was her choice. It would kill me—literally. But I would not let that factor into her decision.

"If you want me to take the blame, I will," I told her meaning every word. Maybe she'd swallowed too much seawater and didn't remember correctly. I didn't care. It was twenty-five years ago. If she loved me now that was fucking fantastic. "I'll do anything."

Petunia sighed and seated herself on a chaise. She twisted her hair in her fingers. I could tell she was trying to figure out what to say. I was jealous of her slim fingers. I would have given almost anything to run my hands through her gorgeous orange curls.

"Umm... I was about to say the same thing," she said with a little giggle. "But I really did show up."

"So did I," I told her, frustrated.

Wait. This was going to get us nowhere. I was in this for the long game—no Super Bowl pun intended. Winning the short game didn't matter at all. Petunia clearly believed what she was saying and so did I. It would hurt nothing to take the blame. Nothing. I loved the Mermaid in front of me with my entire heart and soul. Period.

"You know what?" I asked, feeling a little strange about bending the truth, but if it made the present work, I would happily be the bad guy from the past. "You're right. I got scared and I fucked up. Worst mistake of my life. I am so sorry."

"You are?" she asked, with a small smile pulling at her lips and a sparkle of desire in her eyes.

"I am," I said firmly. "I love you and I will until the day I die. I swear I would have chased you down if I hadn't been stuck in a glass bottle for twenty-five years."

"Was it awful?" Petunia asked, cautiously approaching me and brushing my hair off my forehead.

It felt so good, I could have died happy in this moment. The simple touch of her hand fed my soul.

"It wasn't great," I said, with a chuckle.

She went to remove her hand, but I grabbed her wrist and gently kept it where it was. Her touch was more necessary than oxygen right now.

"You know what?" my Mermaid said, looking at me with desire and adoration. "It was me. I screwed up. I'm so sorry I didn't show up. It was the absolute worst decision I've made in my life. I love you, Delphinus. You're my star in the sky that I haven't been able to see in many years. I'm truly sorry."

I was stunned. I didn't know if she was telling the truth or doing what I'd just done. I was so confused trapped in her seductive web I couldn't remember who didn't show up.

Wait. I did show up, but I was pretty damned sure she didn't remember it that way. Clearly, we were both willing to take the blame for something neither of us believed we did so we could start over. Life. Was. Fucking. Great.

"What do you say, we take my idiot brother's advice and let the past be the past," I suggested, unable to believe I was quoting the dumbass.

Petunia giggled and settled her sexy self in my lap. "Hard to believe Pirate Doug said something that made sense... but yes. The past is the past, never to be repeated."

I pulled her close and breathed her in. Her scent was intoxicating. "Good with me."

"What happened to the sparkle in your eyes—your Genie Star Fire Light?" she asked with concern, raising my chin and staring into my eyes.

"Being stupid and losing you," I told her. It was the truth. Of course, it was only part of the truth. "I've been miserable without you, Mermaid. Are you positive you're ready to give us a second chance?"

"Well, Genie," she said with a raised brow and a lopsided grin that made my heart skip a beat. "I was thinking along the same lines. How do I know you won't leave me again?"

I could ask the same question, but I wouldn't.

"I can give you my word, but I don't believe that will be

enough," I said. "I can grant you three wishes and I would be bound to you for the rest of time."

Petunia wrinkled her nose and shook her head. "I don't want you to be with me unless you want to. This has to be by choice—not magic."

Shit. I sucked at this.

"NO! I meant that I *want* to do that. I would love that. And it's not all altruistic," I added quickly. "It means that you're bound to me too."

"It does?" she asked, pursing her lips in thought. "Sooooo, if I let you grant me three wishes, it's kind of like a permanent no-going-back mating?"

"YES!" I yelled joyfully, wanting to kiss her senseless, but needed her to be on the same page. "I can show my commitment to you and you can show your commitment to me. Forever."

She paused in thought and absently played with my hair. "Well, then you probably need to know I have a career and a family now."

"Here?" I asked with a slight wince. Her cousins were terrifying.

"Yep," she said with a wide grin. "I have my cousins and my pretend dad."

"Pretend dad?" I asked, raising my brow.

Petunia nodded and laughed. "He doesn't actually know I think of him as a dad, but his name is Upton and he's a Pirate and a Sphinx. I adore him."

"I see," I said, loving her delight. "And is this Upton the same Pirate-Sphinx who made the bean salad?"

Petunia gagged. "Umm... yes. That stinky stuff could kill

even an immortal. He's a horrible cook, but he's the best person ever. I promise. And as long as you're good to me, he won't send you to Davy Jones' locker."

"Good to know," I said with a grin. "Do you have a pretend mother too?"

"I most certainly do," she said, pressing her nose to mine. "Yolanda is due to arrive tomorrow. I've haven't met her yet, but she knows all about me and already loves me."

"You're very lovable," I replied.

Petunia looked me right in the eye with an expression of true surprise. "You really think so?"

"I know so. I've loved you since the first second I saw you."

"Wanna know a secret?" she asked, laying her head on my shoulder and snuggling close.

"Always."

"I'm starting to love myself too. I'm worth something," she whispered.

My heart lurched in sorrow. How could this wonderful person not know how amazing she was? Her outside shell was exquisite, but her insides were even lovelier. No matter. I would spend the rest of eternity making sure she was aware how necessary she was.

"You're worth everything to me," I told her. "And if you want to live here with your murderous cousins and your new pretend parents, I'm in. I don't exactly have a home at the moment anyway. Just got out of the bottle a few days ago."

"I seem to remember you talking about your mom," she said.

"Umm... I'd go back into the bottle before I'd live with my mom or gods forbid, my dad."

Petunia's laugh went all through me and I needed her now more than ever.

"You don't want to live on Mount Olympus with your soused diaper-wearing daddy?" she asked with a gleam in her eyes.

"Nope. And my mom is more of a nutbag than my dad."

"But she loves you?" she asked.

"She does," I admitted with a nod. I still couldn't believe my mother had gone to Genie Headquarters and terrorized the elders. That was insanity personified, which was love according to my mom. "Eventually, you'll meet her. She'll love you as much as I do. I'm quite sure she'll come up with some fucking awful nicknames for you. All in the name of love."

"I look forward to it," Petunia said. "Oh, and just so you know, my pretend mom is a Yeti."

"For real?" I asked, impressed.

"Yep and she loves cookies."

"As long as she loves you, I'll love her," I promised. "Ready for your wishes?"

"Now?"

"Yes, now. I want you bound to me for eternity and then I'd be delighted to get into your panties."

"I'm going commando," my Mermaid replied with a delighted smile. "However, I'm good with the rest of it."

I almost passed out since all the blood in my head had traveled to my dick. Closing my eyes and picturing my mother deflated my erection immediately. I needed to be all here to grant my lover her wishes. I wondered what she would want… a mansion? Jewels? A Rolls Royce? She could have whatever her heart desired. I would gladly give her everything I had.

"Your wishes?"

Petunia's adorable nose wrinkled in thought. "Okay, I have the first one!"

I waited to hear what grand gift she wanted.

"I wish for the light to come back to your eyes," she said quietly.

I was flabbergasted. Most wished for objects for themselves—not for others.

"Umm… that will come eventually now that you're back in my life," I told her, resting my chin on the top of her head so she didn't see the tears that had gathered in my eyes. "That one doesn't count. You still have three."

"Well, then… I wish my cousins' business to flourish and grow. The crazy hookers put all their money into it. I need to know they'll always be okay."

"You call them hookers?" I asked shocked.

She looked up and me and winked. "Yep. We can call each other hookers, but you can't."

"Done. Next wish?"

Lost in thought, my Mermaid wiggled around in my lap making it very hard to concentrate. My world-renown package was growing larger by the second. Thankfully, my gal didn't seem to notice… or mind.

"I want Yolanda and Upton to have a fabulous vacation. Let them pick the place," she said, glancing up at me with joy on her face. "And I'd like it to be fully paid for and for as long as they'd like to go."

"That I can do," I promised, wondering where a Yeti and a Pirate-Sphinx would choose. It didn't matter. I would make it happen. "Third wish?"

Petunia blushed and lowered her eyes. This one was going to be good...

"Umm... I was thinking, you know... since we're going to be bonded and all..."

"Yes?" I asked, grinning even though I had no clue what she was going to request.

"Maybewecouldmakethehutbiggerandhaveroom-forababythatwecanstartworkingontonight," she said in one breath.

My joystick was now choking in my pants. I wanted to scream in triumph, but that would not have been cool.

"Can you say that again with spaces in between the words?" I asked, teasing her. "Need to make sure I get your wish correct."

"You're kind of a shit," Petunia said, elbowing me in the gut.

"Your point?"

"No point. Just an observation," she said with a giggle. "Maybe we could make the hut bigger and have a nursery for a baby that we can start working on tonight."

"Done. Done. Done," I said snapping my fingers and making the hut six times the size it was only moments ago. I added five extra bedrooms and five extra baths. We were going to make many, many babies. I put in a playroom and an indoor kiddie pool next to the kitchen. With Petunia being a Mermaid and me being the son of the wasted God of Sea, our little ones would be swimmers from day one.

I also knew how fabulously violent my gal could be, so I put in a fire-retardant gym that also had a boxing ring. I wanted to have an area to kick my pappy's ass when he came to visit. In the space of twenty-four hours, my life had become perfect.

Only one thing could make it better.

"Would it be okay if I kissed you?" I asked.

"Yep, can I straddle you?" Petunia inquired.

"Gods yes," I ground out as she wrapped her legs around my waist and I saw stars. "Can I accidentally on purpose grab your boob?"

"I'd be offended if you didn't," she purred and ran her tongue along my lips. "I was wondering if I could get up close and personal with your famous package?"

I couldn't even speak at this point. All I could do was nod. And I nodded—very enthusiastically.

Petunia did as promised and it was the best day of my life so far. My Johnson was fucking ecstatic. Actually, I was pretty sure all my days now were going to be the best ever.

"How about we take this to the bedroom?" she whispered in my ear, making my balls tighten painfully.

"*The* bedroom or *our* bedroom?" I asked, nipping at her neck.

"Our bedroom," she cried out on a moan of pure pleasure.

"Done. Done and done."

Best. Damned. Day. Of. My. Life.

Ten times. Nuff said.

11
PETUNIA

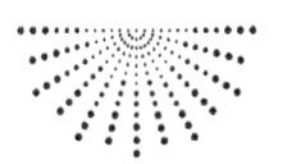

WALKING WAS GOING TO BE A CHALLENGE TODAY, BUT I didn't care. My Genie was a freakin' god in the sack—literally. Well, half-god. I had never been so happy and exhausted in my two hundred years. Of course, I didn't look a day over thirty. Most immortals stopped aging at thirty. My gods, Delphinus was over two-thousand and looked fantastic.

"Duuuuuuuude," Tallulah said with a wink as she joined me on the shore. "Somebody got laid last night."

"Really?" I asked, unable to hide my grin. "Who?"

"Well, I did," Tallulah said with a laugh. "And I *know* you did. Pretty sure everyone within a fifty-mile radius knows that you did."

I could feel my blush travel from my chest and land squarely on my face. I didn't care one little bit. Of course, I was going to ask Delphinus to soundproof our hut ASAP. I had plans to be very busy with my Genie. I didn't need to scare off the human tourists with my *happiness*.

"We're mated," I told my cousin. "I love him and he loves me."

Tallulah tackled me and kissed me all over my face. "I am so delighted! Will you stay here on the Mystical Isle?"

"If that's okay with you, yes," I said hesitantly, realizing that maybe they wouldn't want me here forever.

"Wouldn't have it any other way, hooker," she said, her purple eyes sparkling with joy. "I'd kick your sorry orange tail if you ever tried to leave. And Doug seems very attached to his brother. It might do him good to be around family that isn't freakin' insane."

"Awesome and thank you. Today I'm going to find Charybdis and eliminate her. Delphinus is going with me. I need to wrap up everything from my past so I can move forward," I said. "Avenging my parents will give me peace."

"And not a moment too soon," Tallulah said, flopping back in the sand and letting the early morning sun warm her face. "Our phones have been ringing off the hook! We have reservations booked for the next ten years. Can you believe that shit?"

"Wow," I said, internally grinning from ear to ear. My Genie had granted two of my wishes so far. He was a sexy man of his word—emphasis on *sexy*. "I promise we'll get Charybdis. My business reputation depends on it."

"Speaking of…" Tallulah said, sitting up and brushing the sand from her lavender jeweled bikini top. "Upton and I got up early today and changed up a few things with the business."

"You did?" I asked, confused. "Why?"

"Well, after the *loud* performance last night—*all night*, we figured things were gonna change around here. So, we got a head start."

"Would you like to be more specific?"

"Sure. Arsehole Assassinations compliments of Petunia the Sea Monster Slayer is now called... Arsehole Assassinations compliments of Petunia the Sea Monster Slayer and Delphinus the Genie with the BIG Weenie from the Super Bowl."

My mouth hung open in shock. "You did not," I gasped out, trying not to laugh.

Tallulah cackled and rolled around in the sand. "Nope, but I was tempted. Upton forbade me."

"So, did you really change the name?"

"We did. Your company is now called, Arsehole Assassinations compliments of Petunia the Sea Monster Slayer and Delphinus the Slaughtering Son of the Sea God."

"Kind of long," I pointed out.

"Yep, it was a real bitch getting that to fit on a ballcap, but Upton made the words really tiny and it works," she explained. "Speaking of... where is the Slaughtering Son of the Sea God?"

"He's fixing up the baby nurseries in our hut," I told her with a wide smile.

"You have something to tell me?" Tallulah inquired with a raised brow.

"Not yet, but hopefully soon."

My cousin snapped her fingers and produced two pina coladas.

"It's a little early to start drinking," I said, taking one from her outstretched hand.

"It's five o'clock somewhere," she pointed out.

"That it is," I said, sipping on my drink and wondering how in the seashells I got so very lucky.

"WHAT IN MY PAPPY'S DROOPY DIAPER IS *THAT?*" PIRATE DOUG bellowed in alarm, pointing out to sea.

My cousins, their mates, the Pirates, Delphinus and I had gathered on the beach to make plans to nab Charybdis. Upton had even brought the leftover bean salad. Actually, it was the full bean salad since no one in their right mind would eat it. All was calm until what looked like a comet that had dropped to earth appeared about a mile out at sea and was approaching fast.

"Shite," Upton said, shielding his eyes. "It's so glittery that me durned peepers might be singed."

Snapping her fingers, Tallulah produced sunglasses for all. They were necessary. I'd never seen anything so bright in my life.

"Looks like a star," Misty said, peering out at the incoming mystery.

"Is it an enemy?" Pirate Doug demanded, warming up his hideous voice and getting ready to sing. "I can kill it. Everyone plug your ears."

"NO!" Delphinus yelled, removing his sunglasses and sighing dramatically. "It's not an enemy. It's my mother."

"Crap," I said, looking down at my rumpled sarong and

very aware that my hair was a mess. Delphinus and I had a quickie before the meeting. I didn't mind my cousins knowing. But Delphinus' mom? Shitshitshit. "I need to change."

"No time," he said, pulling me close to his side. "My mother is a hot mess. Adara doesn't notice anyone but herself."

"You sure?" I asked, still feeling weird.

"Positive."

The sparkling star riding on a magic carpet smothered in precious jewels arrived seconds later. Delphinus was correct. There was no time to change. He said his mother loved him, but just in case she was awful to him, I wanted to be here to kick her ass. I knew that female Genies were violent, but I was no slouch in the ass-kicking department. Delphinus had been through enough. I was going to take care of him now.

"I have your back," I whispered.

My Genie looked down at me and grinned. "And I have yours, beautiful. Always."

"Hello," Adara called out as her magic carpet hovered over the shallows, shimmering brighter than the sea on a sunny day. "I'm looking for my Dazzling Cake Penguin. Has anyone seen him?"

"What did she just call you?" I asked, choking back a laugh.

"Don't laugh," he said, letting his head fall back onto his shoulders. "When she finds out about you, you too will have hideous nicknames."

"That's mean," I said, still trying not to laugh.

"All in the name of love," he reminded me and then

raised his hand to wave to his nutty mom. "Hi, Mom. I'm right here."

"Oh, thank the gods, Dazzling Peach Bug."

"And I thought Pirate Slug was bad," Pirate Doug muttered. "I'm glad your wank is large. That's fucking emasculating, brother."

"Yep," Delphinus agreed. "How did you find me here, Mother?"

"I talked to your bum-tamping, crap-bender of a father," she announced, checking her lipstick in a diamond-encrusted mirror. "I think I traumatized him. The hamster-banging, turd-chewing bone-camper was babbling nonsense when I left. However, his mate Wally is FABULOUS! She's going to join my bridge group."

"Shite," Pirate Doug muttered. "Wally's my mum. That doesn't bode well for me getting castrating nicknames."

"Not much my mother does bodes well," Delphinus told his brother. "However, she means well."

I looked at my Genie as he stared at his mom and smiled. You could tell a lot about a man by the way he treated his mother. While Adara certainly seemed certifiable, it was clear that Delphinus loved her. That was enough for me. No matter what embarrassing name she called me, I would love her too.

"Are you still dying, Lovely Mango Bee?" Adara demanded, squinting toward the shore.

Even she had a hard time seeing with all that bling around her.

Wait. What did she just say?

"You're dying?" I shouted, whacking Delphinus in the

back of the head and sending him flying. "When were you going to mention that?"

"I can explain," he said.

"Whoopsy," Adara said with a delighted squeal. "And who might you be, lovely Mermaid?"

Kicking Delphinus' legs out from underneath him as he tried to get up, I then turned to his glittery mom. "I'm Petunia. I'm your son's mate. Apparently, he forgot to tell me he was *dying*," I yelled as my fingers began to spark and shoot flames willy nilly. "Would you like to enlighten me?"

"Ohhhhh, you're a vicious one, Jolly Llama Pancake," Adara said, clapping her hands together with glee. "You have my full permission kick Bashful Angel Cow's tushy when he gets out of line."

Now I was confused. She was crazier than Poseidon. What the hell was she talking about?

"Umm... let's back up a bit," I suggested.

"Certainly, Exceptional Banana Strudel Kitty," Adara said, pulling a Genie bottle out of her Chanel bag and placing it on her floating magic carpet. "Which part?"

"The part about Delphinus dying?" I prompted her.

"Delicious Coco Flamingo," she called out to her son. "Look at your mother. NOW."

Delphinus warily got to his feet just in case I was going to take him out again. He shrugged his broad shoulders, walked to the water's edge and stared at his mom.

"Excellent," she sang as she picked up the bottle and shook it violently. "I have a surprise for you, Yummy Gummy Bear and for your lovely vicious Mermaid, Precious Koala Butt."

"Surprises are not good," I muttered as I walked to the water's edge and joined the omitter that I'd mated with. "So, you're dying? Might have been something you wanted to tell me."

"Would you not of mated with my Thrilling Lollypop Papaya if you'd known?" Adara inquired, narrowing her eyes at me dangerously.

The crazy overly-Botoxed Genie didn't scare me. The thought of losing the man I loved with my heart and soul did. With an enormous eye roll and a lifted middle finger aimed at Adara, I growled. "Of course, I would have, Lemony Sugar Monkey Balls. I love the jackhole. And your assumption was incredibly rude. I. Don't. Like Rude. You feel me?"

"You are FANTASTIC!" Adara squealed. "Poseidon—that scum-sipping, ass-blister—said you were, but he's usually so intoxicated, I never know what to believe. And just so you know, my Dirty Apple Turnover Lizard didn't tell you because he must truly love you. Right, Squishy Radish Puppy?"

"Umm… Mom," Delphinus said, shaking his head. "You really have to tamp that nickname shit back."

"My bad. Sorry, Scrunchy Cinnamon Coffee Bean. I'll work on it."

"Start talking," I said to my Genie as he eyed me with amusement.

"You would have mated with me if you'd known I was dying?" he asked.

"Yes," I snapped, ready to deck him again, but I needed to hear the whole story first. "I love you no matter what."

"My Genie Star Fire Light was going out because I found my true mate and she didn't want me."

"What kind of idiot wouldn't want you?" I demanded, wanted to kick her ass. I mean, I was devastated that he had a true mate who wasn't me, but...

"It's you," he said softly so the others wouldn't hear. "When you didn't show up for our mating by the ocean, I basically lost a few screws. I did some wildly stupid shit like showing my pecker to the Universe—not to mention I stole the Mona Lisa which is hanging in our bedroom now. Anyway, when you said you still loved me, I refused to use my life or lack thereof as a bargaining chip. You are too good of a person to do that to and I love you too much. I needed you to want me because you loved me—plain and simple."

"So how long do you have?" I asked as tears filled my eyes and I wrapped my arms around the Genie I adored.

"Well," Delphinus said with a chuckle that I could feel vibrating through his body. "I'd have to say a few million more years."

"What?" I snapped, pulling back and glaring at him. This was not a freakin' joke.

"When a Genie like me joins forever with his true mate, his Genie Star Fire Light comes back. Look in my eyes, Petunia. See what you do to me."

I did. In Delphinus' eyes I saw his Star Fire and I also saw my reflection in them. His love for me burned clear and bright. It was far more beautiful than any star in the night sky.

"Wait," I said, thinking back through all I'd just learned. "The ocean? What do you mean *our mating by the ocean?*"

"That's where we were supposed to meet," Delphinus said. "It was more romantic by the ocean than in Vegas. I wanted everything to be perfect for you."

"I was in Vegas," I gasped out as my skin felt hot and icy cold at the same time.

"But I sent you a message," he said, paling. "I'm gonna kill him."

"Yoohoo," Adara called out waving the bottle to get our attention.

Delphinus was positively glowing with rage and I was completely confused.

"I don't have time for a surprise, Mother," he roared, causing all on the beach to back away from him except me.

I was beginning to realize that neither of us had lied about not showing up. But we had both lied last night so that we could have a second chance at love. We *had* both shown up to our original mating. We'd simply shown up in the wrong place. Twenty-five wasted years of heartache. What the ever-loving heck?

"You have time for this *surprise,*" Adara hissed.

Her eyes glowed so brightly that I had to look away. It was like staring straight into the sun. The furious Genie opened the bottle and a man fell out onto her magic carpet. With a sharp slice of her hand through the air that caused a shimmering silver explosion, the man screamed in agony and went from tiny to full-sized. "Would you like to explain to my son what you did, you tainted nut-biscuit, dick-nosed rectum blossom, sequined crotch box of a soon to be dead Genie?"

"Holy shite," Pirate Doug said in admiration. "You cuss better than a sailor."

"Thank you," Adara said, gracing Pirate Doug with a smile so brilliant it twinkled. "I give lessons on Tuesdays. I'll mark you down as a new student."

"Excellent," Pirate Doug shouted. "I shall bring rare rum that I pilfered from my pappy."

"I'll join ye as well," Upton said. "I can bring me bean salad."

"I love bean salad!" Adara said. "A good shart attack is excellent for my figure."

"Excuse me," Delphius ground out, still glowing and sparking with rage. "As lovely as it is that we're all bonding, I'm quite interested to know why my *old buddy* Botein is here."

"Oh yes," Adara said and zapped the living daylights out of this Botein character. "I believe the pie-eating crotch knob would like to share something with you and your lovely Cushy Muffin Buffalo. Am I correct, Botein?"

Adara once again zapped the living daylights out of the Genie.

"Speak," Delphinus demanded. "What have you got to say?"

I took my Genie's glowing hand in my own and held tight. His anger didn't scare me. My goal was to calm him. Glancing over at me he gave me a tight smile. Something awful was about to go down. I could feel it in my tail.

"My Crunchy Chocolate Chip Bunny said speak," Adara roared, making the ground tremble beneath our feet.

"It was my fault," Botein choked out as Adara zapped him again. "I followed the directions of the elders and didn't make your mate aware of the change of venue."

"You did WHAT?" I shouted as pissed off as my mate now. "Can I zap him?"

"Be my guest," Adara said as I threw a fireball at the scum who almost killed my mate by denying him his true love.

"*Why?* Why would you do such a thing?" Delphinus ground out in a voice that matched his fury. "You were supposed to be my friend."

"May I cut in here?" Pirate Doug inquired.

Delphinus was so furious he could barely speak. Not a problem. We were a team now.

"Umm... okay," I said, wondering if he was going to sing and blow Botein to bits. Just in case, I wiggled my nose and conjured up enough noise-canceling earphones for the whole group.

"I watch a lot of the detective shows on TV," Pirate Doug told the slightly confused crowd. "I have a theory as to why the earwax-eating, sphincter douche-waffle committed such a heinous crime."

"That description was wonderful," Adara praised Pirate Doug. "You will receive an A in my class most definitely."

Pirate Doug grinned from ear to ear and gave Adara a gallant bow. "I do believe that Botein was insanely jealous of my brother's gargantuan one-eyed willy. Not many men in this Universe have wands of life like my brother and myself.

Having an extraordinary peen like Delpenis and I have makes other men do evil deeds. Taco hammers the size of ours..."

"Does this have a point?" I asked, shaking my head. The Pirate could go on for days when talking about his member.

Pirate Doug appeared completely confused for about a minute and a half while we waited for his brain to catch up to his story.

"Yes!" he said. "It does. The shite stain on the rug tried to ruin Delpenis' life because he was furious that he didn't have an outstanding pecker like my brother. The arsehole even went so far as to separate true mates knowing it would kill Delpenis."

"My name is not Delpenis," Delphinus said flatly.

"Right. My bad." Pirate Doug said. "My work here is done. We can send this to the jury for a verdict."

"Is that true?" I asked the cowering man on the carpet. If it was, he was a bigger idiot than my cousin-in-law.

"No," Botein snarled, eyeing me with hatred and disgust. "It is time for the Genie race to become pure. No more crossbreeding with lesser beings. Delphinus is the strongest of the Genies. We're making a super race of our kind. I did what I had to do."

"You're a speciest," I shouted and nailed him with another fireball. "You almost killed the man I love because you have no tolerance of other species. You totally suck."

I finished off my tirade with yet one more fireball.

"What should I do with him?" Adara inquired as she grabbed Botein by the scruff of the neck and shook him like a rag doll. "This piece of hamster-humping dingleberry tried to kill my son. I say a life for a life."

"NO," Delphinus said, pointing at Botein and sending a stream of magic so strong, the evil Genie convulsed in agony and passed out. "He will go back into the bottle after he reveals the names of the others involved in this deadly idiocy. Death is far too kind for scum like him. He will rot in the bottle for all eternity."

"Good one, Delpenis," Pirate Doug congratulated his sibling. "Remind me never to get on your bad side."

"I know who the others are," Adara said with an evil little grin. "I've de-balled them and put them in bottles. They will not be causing you trouble ever again, Yummy Gummy Bear."

Shoving Botein back into the bottle, she dropped the glass prison back into her bag.

"My work here is done," she said, bestowing all with a blinding smile. "I'll expect my son and his lovely ballsy Mermaid for dinner next Friday. Am I clear?"

"You are," I said with a smile as I held tight to Delphinus. "We will be there."

With that she disappeared in a blast of the shiniest glitter I'd ever witnessed. My body sagged with a relief so great, I almost dropped to the sand. Were the surprises finally over? Could Delphinus and I start our life together now? This had been one hell of a day so far and it wasn't even noon.

"Incoming," Upton shouted with joy as he pointed out to the ocean. "Me cackle fruit is swimmin' in! Yolanda loves me bean salad. Lucky fer me love, I have leftovers."

My exhaustion left me in a flash and I searched the

horizon for my pretend mom with the orange braided beard. This was a surprise that I wanted. All the puzzle pieces of my life were about to be connected.

As I scanned the water, my stomach clenched in terror. The sun slid behind darkening clouds and the waves in the sea grew choppy and dangerous. The crystal clear, teal-blue water turned gray and murky and the gentle ocean breeze was no longer gentle.

The feeling of déjà vu was unnerving and dreadful.

"NO, NO, NO," Upton roared.

We all watched in horror as Yolanda got pulled into a deadly whirlpool.

Without a second thought, I sprinted to the ocean and dove in. I felt my tail form and I swam faster than I ever had in my life.

Charybdis had taken the life of my mother. The was no way in hell she was going to take the life of my pretend mother.

Today was the sea monster's last.

12
DELPHINUS

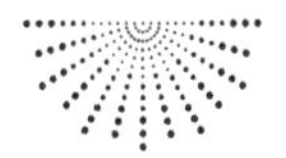

I'd never been so fucking scared in my two-thousand years. Watching my reason for breathing dive into the deadly water was enough to take centuries off my life. I'd just gotten my life back, there was no way in the Seven Seas I was going to watch it end.

The mission was difficult. The outcome? Potentially deadly. It was time to go with my gut. With no time to lose, I rolled into action. Being part Genie and part god had to be good for something. I just prayed to my soused sire that it would be enough. Unintentionally, I'd failed Petunia before. That was not going to happen again.

"Bean salad," I roared. "Give me the damned bean salad."

"Seriously?" Pirate Doug asked, arming himself to the teeth. "It smells like arse."

"Yes," I commanded, kicking off my combat boots and keeping my eye on my Mermaid. "Pirates, man your ship.

Sail immediately. Everyone else, get your weapons and hit the water. We kill the beast TODAY!"

"Delpenis," Pirate Doug shouted as he tossed me the bean salad and then began swimming out to his ship. "If you bite it today, I want you to know that I'm proud to have a brother with such a large taco hammer. I will never forget you, my man."

There was no time to punch him in the head. I'd get to that later. Right now, I had more pressing business.

"May Poseidon be with ye, fake son-in-law," Upton said, touching my back. "We need to save me mate and our girl."

"I have every intention of doing so, sir," I promised.

"Yar a worthy scallywag," Upton said as he took the form of a Sphinx.

I was awed and flabbergasted at the enormous stone creature he became. Lumbering into the water the huge Sphinx began to search for his loves. I could only hope that I was indeed worthy of his trust.

"What are you going to do?" Tallulah yelled as she dove into the water and began to swim.

"Win," I said as I ran so fast toward the ocean, I knew I couldn't be seen by the human eye. "I'm going to fucking win."

"Delpenis and Pirate Dong forever," my brother shouted into the wind as he set sail. "Two well-hung brothers who will WIN!"

I took the briefest of seconds to smile at the proclamation of my idiot brother. He was an imbecile, but he was my imbecile. Maybe I wouldn't punch him too hard in the head when we were done.

Nah, I'd nail him.

Petunia

THE SEA HAD GROWN SO DARK, I COULDN'T SEE ANYTHING IN front of me. I didn't care. I swam with a determination borne of love for a person I'd never met. The raw agony in Upton's voice empowered me. I was so furious that I hadn't found and killed the sea monster yet. If I'd been more diligent this wouldn't be happening.

Popping my head above the waves, I searched for signs of my pretend mom. I'd baked ten dozen chocolate chip seaweed cookies for Yolanda. I had no intention of those damned cookies going to waste.

"Yolanda," I screamed over the roar of the crashing waves. "Where are you?"

No answer.

"I'll save you, Fake Mom," I snarled. "I promise."

Diving back under, I felt something grab my tail. Before I turned and blew it up, I felt Delphinus' familiar hand on my back. Shit, he was a Genie. He couldn't swim like I could. Flipping over and preparing to drop-kick his beloved ass back to shore, I gasped.

My Genie wasn't just a Genie.

The top half of my lover was as I expected, but the bottom half… not so much. Where his legs should have been was the most magnificent tail I'd ever seen. It shimmered like a star even in the murky and now black ocean.

Delphinus was the son of the Sea God. The proof swam right next to me.

"Have you seen her?" he asked, taking my hand and diving deep.

"You can talk underwater?" I asked, surprised.

"Apparently," he said with a shocked laugh. "What does Yolanda look like?"

"Umm... a Yeti," I said, not knowing much else. "But her beard is braided and dyed orange to match my hair."

"Sounds lovely," Delphinus said without an ounce of sarcasm in his voice.

Gods, I couldn't love the man more.

The ocean churned and tossed us around like sand in a windstorm. We kept swimming. I was surprised and so grateful that my Genie was as strong a swimmer as me—maybe even stronger.

"Whirlpool ahead," Delphinus growled.

"I'm going in," I said, picking up speed.

"Going with you," he yelled, shooting ahead of me.

"You could die," I told him, catching up.

"I'd rather die with you than live without you."

Well, that was certainly romantic. He was totally getting laid tonight if we made it out in one piece.

"I love you," I said as we headed into a watery hell.

"I love you too, Mermaid. Let's kill some shit."

Shit was the operative word. Charybdis was a piece of shit—murderous shit. She'd taken out my parents a century ago and now she was going to try to take out everyone I loved.

Not gonna happen.

At least I hoped not.

Today was not a good day to die.

Delphinus

CHUNKS OF COLORFUL CORAL ZOOMED PAST US AS WE SWAM in a zigzag line to avoid being taken out by flying debris. I'd seen my share of shitshows in my time, but this was epic.

"Oh gods, no," Petunia cried out as an unattached orange braid floated by.

She grabbed it, kissed it and tucked it into her bikini top. Even underwater I could see she was crying.

"On three we go in," I yelled, swatting away a school of terrified fish.

My Mermaid nodded and her orange eyes lit with a fire I'd never seen. It was scary, hot and damned impressive. My gal was now Petunia the Sea Monster Slayer and I was Delphinus the Slaughtering Son of the Sea God.

"Should I blow it up?" she asked. "Might be easier to get in."

While my Mermaid was correct, she was also incorrect. "No, if Yolanda's alive, she's probably weak. An explosion could end her," I said, not liking the potential truth of my statement. But sugarcoating anything right now was counterproductive.

Petunia nodded curtly and prepared herself.

"One. Two. Three." I finished the count and we exploded into action.

Going through the outer wall of the whirlpool caused searing pain like I'd never felt—like hot knives ripping through my skin. Glancing over in concern at my partner, I watched in awe as she gritted her teeth and kept going. Holding on to Petunia's hand, I swam as hard as I could. My gal was a work of deadly art in the ocean. I'd never been so proud of her.

"There," she shouted, pointing to a bizarrely calm part of the sea in the middle of the watery melee. "I see her."

It was if we'd entered the eye of the storm in a hurricane. No crashing waves. No flying debris. And unfortunately, no Charybdis in sight. Surrounding the serene area we'd entered was a raging tempest. The eerie quiet was unsettling and didn't bode well for a happy ending.

However, Petunia was right. Yolanda was lying on a large rock, battered and bloody. I just hoped she was alive.

"Grab her," I said tersely. "I'll keep watch for the monster."

"Will she make it back through the wall?" Petunia asked frantically, speeding toward her fake mom.

"Don't know," I answered truthfully as I scanned the area for the piece of shit I had come to kill. "But she certainly won't make it if she stays here."

"Roger that," Petunia said.

"Oh fuck," I yelled as a horror I hadn't expected caught my eye.

"What?" Petunia shouted back as she gently took Yolanda into her arms.

I couldn't believe what I was seeing. It was sick and so inhumane, I had to tamp back my need to incinerate the entire ocean. There were five emaciated and chained immortals at the bottom of the whirlpool. Their eyes looked dead and defeated. And their bodies? Horrifying—near skeletal and beaten terribly.

"There are more," I snarled as I headed to the bottom of the whirlpool. "We have to save them."

The poor souls most likely wouldn't make it out alive, but they were immortal. At the very least they had a *chance* of surviving. I was going to make sure they had that chance.

Petunia

I DIDN'T KNOW WHAT DELPHINUS MEANT. HOW COULD THERE be more?

"I'll be back for you," I whispered to an unconscious Yolanda, laying her gently back on the rock and kissing her forehead.

She was every bit as beautiful as I'd imagined—and every bit as hairy. Her beard was a bloody mess, but I could see the dyed orange part through the blood. Her eyes were closed and her breathing was shallow. I hadn't known that Yetis could breathe underwater, but I didn't know much about my fake mom's kind. I was just wildly grateful for any favor right now.

"I promise I'll be right back."

Time was of the essence. Charybdis was nowhere to be found, but I was sure she'd be back. Swimming like my life depended on it—which it actually did—to the bottom of the whirlpool, I froze. Closing my eyes tight and then opening them again, I tried to understand what I was seeing. It made no sense.

My skin felt icy, but a fiery rage burned in my chest making it hard to breathe.

"We have to save them," Delphinus ground out as he tore through the chains with his bare hands.

Glancing back over his shoulder, he stared at me.

"Help me, Petunia. We don't have much time," he insisted and went back to work.

I couldn't move. I simply stared. The scene was like a dream come true combined with the worst nightmare I'd ever had in my life. They were here—all this time they'd been here. Chained and tortured. Death would have been kinder.

Was this real? Were my eyes playing tricks on me?

"Petunia, NOW," Delphinus roared as he freed my mother and father from what had to have been hell underwater for a century.

Snapping to attention, I swam to the man and woman who bore me and wondered if they would recognize me. I knew them the moment I saw them even though they were a mere shell of who they'd been.

"I've got you," I choked out through my tears, gently taking my parents' hands and leading them to relative safety.

Nothing was safe right now. Nothing at all.

Delphinus led the other three to the rock where Yolanda lay barely alive. I was almost in a state of shock. I didn't have any clue what to do with myself. I vacillated between a happiness that seemed to swallow me whole and a fury that consumed me with a rage I was unaware I was capable of.

"Petunia," Delphinus said, looking at me with worry. "You have to stay with me. We need to get these people out of here. Now."

"My parents," I whispered in a voice that sounded far away even to my own ears. "These are my parents."

"*What?*" Delphinus asked, staring at the gaunt man and woman whose hands I held. "Your parents?"

I nodded and gave the man I loved a watery smile. "You saved my parents."

Delphinus closed his eyes for a moment and then bowed to my parents. "We aren't safe yet," he said flatly. "We have to get them to shore. The sooner the better."

"Yes," I said. "Can you swim with Yolanda? She's out and needs help."

"I can," he said, turning his attention to the other three people that had been chained. "Are there more?"

"No," my father said, touching my face in disbelief. "Charybdis only kept the five of us to torture. I don't know why. She eats the humans she captures."

"Soon she won't be eating anything," I snarled, placing my hand over my father's. "Soon she'll be dead."

Delphinus broke in and suggested something different. "As much as I want her dead, we have to get everyone to safety. We'll have to come back for the monster."

"You're right," I said, hoping that everyone made it through the outer wall of the whirlpool.

"Well, fuck," Delphinus growled. "Change of plans."

Unfortunately, my Genie was correct. There would be

no time to get everyone to shore. Time was a luxury we no longer had.

Charybdis had arrived.

She was pissed and one of the most heinous beings I'd ever laid eyes on.

However, the sea monster didn't know pissed.

Nope.

But she was about to learn and it would be the last thing she ever did.

Delphinus

WITH A SCREAM OF ANGER THAT CAME FROM THE MOST RAGE-filled part of my Mermaid, she jetted forward like a bullet out of a machine gun. Again, centuries of my life disappeared. With a quick glance to make sure Petunia's parents, fake mom and the other three were out of the line of fire, I followed the love of my immortal life into the fray.

Yes. We were immortal. However, beheading killed everyone.

Charybdis had teeth that looked like razor-sharp tusks coming out of what I guessed was her stomach. It was hard to tell. I'd never seen anything like it. The body was a muddy color and shaped like a deformed octopus with hundreds of tentacles. The monster's appendages shot streams of a noxious dark magic. On the very top of her bulbous body was a knob with eyes. They were narrowed to slits and oozing.

This was fucking bad.

"Stay here," I instructed the group as I reached deep inside for magic I hoped I possessed. As a Genie, I was limited. As the son of Poseidon, I wasn't. I was about to test those limits.

"To your left," Petunia shouted.

I ducked a deadly stream of magic headed my way. "Petunia, go for the head."

"It's one big head," she shouted back throwing massive fireball after massive fireball.

I was impressed that she was strong enough to keep fire alive underwater, but the time to admire my Mermaid wasn't now.

"On the top," I grunted as I got hit by a stream of black magic. It burned right through my skin leaving the bone exposed. "Knob on the top."

"Blob on the slop?" she questioned, confused as the monster screamed with such anger, I was sure my eardrums would pop.

"Close and kind of makes sense," I yelled over the thrashing water. "KNOB ON THE TOP."

"Got it," Petunia snarled and she swam so fast she disappeared.

With a very heartfelt and quick prayer for Petunia's safety sent to my intoxicated father, I went for it. There was no other choice.

Petunia

THE FEELING OF RAGE WAS TANGLED WITH IMMORTAL FEAR for Delphinus' life. He was helping me fight my battle and he could die. That was unacceptable. I was going for the knob on the top and only death could stop me.

Of course, stopping me was Charybdis' goal. Unfortunately, she was very good at getting what she wanted. She'd had my parents for a hundred years.

"Die," the monster hissed, shooting black magic now coupled with poisonous darts.

It was a very good thing that I'd done Jazzercise for the last several decades. I wasn't as limber as Upton, but I had moves. Weaving, flipping and dodging the darts, I got close enough to her tiny head to do my business.

"I've got your back," Delphinus roared as he swam up behind me.

And that was the last thing I heard him say.

With a bellow that would live in my nightmares for eternity, the disgusting piece of shit shot a massive poisonous dart that hit my Genie in his beautiful chest. Delphinus' eyes grew wide for a brief moment before his battered and lifeless body began to sink to the ocean floor.

My heart shattered permanently. I had nothing left. Silently, I begged Poseidon to send someone to save Yolanda, my parents and the others. I was sure that Upton was on his way. He would find them.

I had nothing left to live for. Maybe today was a good day to die. As long as I took Charybdis with me, I simply didn't care anymore.

"Get ready to say goodbye, you piece of murdering shit,"

I snarled as I dive-bombed her head with a vengeance that came from having lost everything.

In the end, it had been easy. The monster had never witnessed savagery like mine. She got her shots in and damaged me to the extent I was sure I was a goner. That didn't matter. Her head was in my hands. It was no longer attached to her blubbery body. She would never harm anyone again.

I was just devasted that I'd been too late. Dying would be a blessing. I could be with my Genie. Closing my eyes, I let go. My body ached so much I wasn't sure where the pain was coming from.

Sleep. I just wanted to sleep.

Delphinus

"OPEN YOUR EYES," I SHOUTED AT THE CRUMPLED BODY OF MY Mermaid. "For the love of the gods, please open your eyes."

Petunia the Sea Monster Slayer had indeed slayed the monster, but had she depleted herself so badly she wouldn't survive?

Upton had arrived on the scene with the Mermaids, their mates and the Pirates. Once they assessed what was happening, they quickly and expertly moved all to shore. I'd been hit by a massive dart, but being the son of a god had saved me. Clearly, Petunia hadn't known this. She'd gone after Charybdis like a woman who had nothing left to live for.

I hated myself right now. This was my fault. By the time I'd regained my strength, it was too late. My reason for living was barely alive.

"The stars are coming out," Upton said as he squatted down beside me on the shore.

We were surrounded by all the people who loved my Mermaid. Yolanda had made it as had Petunia's parents and the other prisoners. I was happy for them, but part of me hated them for surviving. It was wrong. Petunia would not be okay with my train of thought at the moment.

"I don't care about the stars," I told Upton tersely. "They mean nothing."

"Well, they mean a lot to me little Mermaid," Upton said. "Petunia loves the stars in the sky just like she loves ye."

"Don't you mean loved?" I snapped, willing her to come to.

"Nay, I mean love," Upton corrected me. "Yolanda? Do ye have the bean salad?"

What the fuck was happening here? Petunia was dying in front of me and Upton was concerned about *bean salad*?

"Upton, with all due respect," I ground out through clenched teeth. "I don't give a shit about your bean salad. Unless you know how to wake Petunia up, I'd appreciate some privacy."

"Aye, lad," Upton said with a chuckle. "I believe I do, but yar gonna have to do yer part as well."

Was he crazy? Probably, but if the Pirate-Sphinx knew something I didn't I was all ears.

"Fine. Tell me what to do."

Upton smiled and took a spoonful of the vile-smelling

salad from his mate. "Me bean salad has magic in it," he explained. "It can help bring our girl back. I make it with love."

"Then feed it to her," I insisted, moving out of the way so Upton could do his thing.

"I will, laddie," he promised. "But the little swimmin' hooker will need more than just a magic bean potion. Are ye ready?"

"Yes," I said and then paused. "Ready for what?"

"Petunia has always searched for the star in the sky that ye can see in yar peripheral vision, but then when ye look upon it, it disappears. She told me that everything would be okay if she could just see that star. A star burning bright fer someone it loves is some fine medicine. Stardust doesn't hurt either."

My smile came slowly, but when it landed it was full. That I could do. I was a star. I would be a star until the day I burned out and left this Universe. If my love wanted to see every damned star in the sky, I would make it happen.

Closing my eyes and calling out to the stars above, I felt my body begin to levitate. I let the heat and the brightness consume me and I laughed as I felt the shimmer and magical sparkle shoot from my now reformed body. Rising high into the sky, I sent love and healing magic back down to the most important woman in my life.

Looking down on the scene far below, I watched as Upton put the bean salad into Petunia's mouth. She sat right up, punched him in the head and spit out the rancid concoction. I laughed with joy, sending iridescent silver sparks out into the night sky. They gently rained down on my beautiful Mermaid. She looked up and gasped.

"Delphinus," she whispered, pointing at me.

I twinkled for her and sent down another shower of stardust. Her eyes filled with tears and she reached for me.

"Come back to me," Petunia called out. "I don't want to live without you."

"Aye little swimmin' hooker," Upton said, putting his arm around her and hugging her tight. "Yer scallywag is alive and well. The dingy dangler just wanted ye to see that star ye've been tryin' to find."

"He's alive?" she asked, still staring at me.

"Yep," Upton replied. "He'll be down shortly."

Petunia blew me a kiss. Her smile was the most beautiful thing I'd ever seen. I'd twinkle for her a little longer to make sure she got her wish. After all, I was a Genie.

Wishes were my specialty.

EPILOGUE

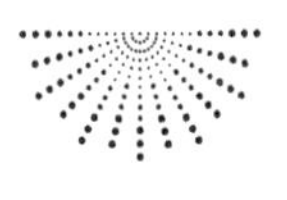

PETUNIA

Six Months Later

Looking down at my growing belly, I giggled. Life had seemed hopeless for so long and now it was dang near perfect.

"How are ye feelin'?" Upton asked as he handed me our morning report.

Business was fantastic. After the news of us taking Charybdis out, we were overrun with lucrative missions. I'd worked in the field for a while, but I was in the office now for a few months. My virile, hot, sexy Genie had knocked me up. Again, life was freakin' fantastic.

"Awesome," I told him. "Starving," I added.

"Yolanda made some bean salad if ye be wantin' some," he offered.

"Umm… thanks, but no," I said, trying not to gag. While I would be forever grateful for the magical healing properties of Upton's bean salad, I hoped to never have it near my lips again. I could taste that crap for weeks and I'd only had a spoonful.

"Alrighty then," Upton said, dancing a little jig around my office in the lodge. "Me and me cackle fruit are all packed and ready to go on our vacation! I want to thank ye for givin' us such a lovely gift," he said, bestowing a sweet kiss on my cheek.

"It's from Delphinus and me," I reminded him. "Where did you decide to go?"

"Disney World!" Yolanda announced with glee, entering the office with a bowl of coconut chunks and pineapple and placing it in front of me. "I'm just so excited."

"That sounds great," I said, giving my furry fake mom a hug.

I was curious how they would get around Disney World undetected, but I figured they had that covered. All of my parents were getting along grandly. My fake mom and dad had chosen names for themselves so it wouldn't be confusing. Upton went by PopPop and Yolanda was partial to Hairy Mimi. It was weird and wonderful... and weird.

"Your mamma and daddy are doing real well," Yolanda told me in her low melodic voice, tying a napkin around my neck like I was five. "They've been thinking about joining us in Disney World."

"They have?" I asked, surprised.

My mom and dad's healing had been a slow process. Even though they were immortal, they'd been horridly tortured by Charybdis for so long it was taking time. As it turned out, Yolanda was a trained nurse and helped all five that had been captured and held prisoner back to health.

Although, she had a very special bond with my mom and dad. It made tears come to my eyes just thinking about it. I cried a lot. Pregnancy hormones could do that to a Mermaid.

"I love you guys so much," I blubbered, wiping my nose with my bib. "I just love you. So much. Like so much love."

"We love you too, sugar," Yolanda said with a smile. "You're my little sunshine."

"Thank you," I said, shoving the pineapple and coconut into my mouth even though I was still crying. I was also hungry.

"There you are," Tallulah said, entering my office and setting a coconut cream pie on my desk.

"Is that for me?" I inquired, eyeing it with desire and wiping my tears away.

"Yep," she said with a laugh. "You eat as much as a lodge full of guests. Thank gods for Mermaid metabolism or you'd be the size of the lodge."

I considered zapping her but decided to eat the pie instead. Besides, she was correct. Our grocery bill was completely out of control. My Genie thought it was hilarious that I could eat more than he could. I didn't think it was funny at all. I'd drop-kicked his laughing ass right out of our hut last night when he'd commented on my adoration of buttery coconut bars.

I was serious about my desserts.

"We're gonna finish packin'," Upton said. "Yar two little hookers be good lassies."

As Upton and Yolanda left the office hand in hand, Tallulah shook her head in defeat. As many times as we'd tried to teach the Pirates not to call us hookers, they just couldn't seem to do it. In the end we'd decided as long as they used it as an endearment, we wouldn't remove any appendages.

"Is everything okay?" I asked, wanting to lick the pie tin, but deciding to wait until I was alone. I still had a little bit of pride left.

"It's great. Delphinus and Doug just got back from visiting Poseidon."

"How'd that go?" I asked, foregoing my pride and licking the tin.

"Well," Tallulah said. "Apparently Poseidon's feelings were hurt because Del gave Doug a wish and enhanced his doink."

"Are you shitting me?" I asked with a laugh.

"I shit you not," she replied with an eye roll. "Not real clear on what actually went down, but I did hear that when they left Mount Olympus, the diaper-wearing dolt couldn't sit down due to his new and improved pecker."

"Shut up," I squealed with laughter. "Did Delphinus fix it?"

"I did not," the love of my life said, walking into our office and dropping his gorgeous frame down on the couch. "I tried. I offered him another wish to fix his grossly overrated miscalculation of dong size, but the dumbass refused."

"On that repulsive note, I'm out," Tallulah said shaking her head and leaving the office. "Men are idiots."

"Are you serious about Poseidon?"

"Serious as a fart attack," he said with a chuckle.

"Umm… you've been hanging out with Pirate Doug too much," I told him.

"Correct," Delphinus agreed. "I think I should remedy that by hanging out with only you."

"I like that idea," I said, joining him on the couch and cuddling close. "I've thought of some names."

"For our baby?" he asked with a shit-eating grin.

"For our daughter," I replied and watched as his eyes grow wide.

"We're having a little girl?"

I nodded. "We are. Yolanda's also a midwife and can tell the sex of the baby just by touching my stomach."

"Amazing," Delphinus whispered, placing his hand on my stomach reverently. "I love our baby so much already. I can't wait to meet her."

"Me too," I said with a happy sigh.

"Names?" he asked, rubbing my tummy.

"Well, I only have one."

"Let's hear it."

I smiled and pressed my lips to his. "I want to call her Vega."

"That's one of the brightest stars in the Universe," Delphinus said, pleased.

"Yep. This little girl is going to shine," I told him.

"If she's anything like her mom she'll be the most beautiful thing in existence—part Mermaid, part Genie and part god."

"Holy hell and seashells," I muttered as it all sank in. "That's a heavy load."

"I agree," my Genie said. "But she has two parents who

love her to the stars and back. She's going to be just fine. Not to mention, my mother will be thrilled with that name. She already has a notebook full of nicknames for her first grandchild."

"Oh shit," I said, giggling. "But it's all from love."

"That it is, my Mermaid. You hungry?" he asked with a lopsided grin.

"I am," I said, squinting at him. "But not for food…"

"Are you saying what I think you're saying?" Delphinus asked, as his Super Bowl famous package perked up.

"I do believe I am," I said, removing my bikini top.

Regularly my knockers were spectacular, but right now they were positively obscene. My Genie loved them. In fact, I was fairly sure he forgot I had eyes since his were glued to my girls.

"I'm ready when you are," he said, stripping down so fast I barely saw him move.

"Lock the door," I said, tearing off my sarong and making quick work of my thong. "I'd hate to traumatize anyone with our *happiness*."

"Our happiness is ours," Delphinus said as he locked the door and began to stalk me like prey.

It was all kinds of perfect—just like him. Oh, he would still get his ass booted every once in a while especially if he gave me crap about buttery coconut bars, but I loved him. Completely. I loved my Genie-god with my entire heart and soul and he loved me with his.

Ten times.

Ten freakin' times.

For a two-thousand-year-old Genie, he was a dang sex machine.

Life. Was. Freakin'. Awesome.

And the best was yet to come.

THE END... FOR NOW

READ THE NEXT BOOK IN THE SERIES! JINGLE ME BALLS

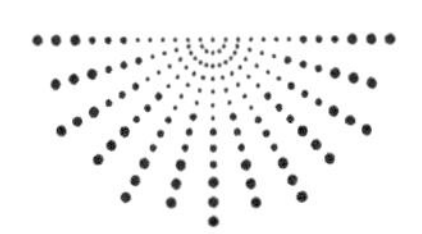

SEA SHENANIGANS, BOOK 6

Get your copy here!

JINGLE ME BALLS

What in the salty seas could be more important than *presents* at Christmas time?

Nothing. Absolutely nothing.

Tis' Christmas time on Mystical Isle and just like the fat bastard in red, I've made a list and now I shall check it...*twice*. Yeah, twice. I might wear a diaper, but I'm not an arse.

Battle the human women in sweatpants and snow boots for electronics on Black Friday. Check.

Cover each palm tree in lights even though the Mermaids insist they look phallic. Check. By the way, what does phallic mean? Never mind. Check.

Moving on.

Weave a Christmas tale during family story time on the beach, have a family portrait made in the special sweaters I pilfered, and write a letter to Santa. I mean, fat bastard… Check.

Planning activities that may end in bloodshed. Check. That's what I call a yuletide win, so check-check.

The Mermaids have baked lovely Christmas cookies that will go wonderfully with the rum in my diaper. And everyone has voted to veto caroling since Pirate Doug has a singing voice that can kill… literally. The present exchange would be ruined if everyone was dead. Could my days be merrier or brighter? Uh, no. Check.

It seems I have *everything* under control and Christmas on Mystical Isle will be unforgettable, or I'm not the Well-Hung God of the Sea, Poseidon.

And I am. Check.

Go here to get the book!!!

MORE IN THIS SERIES

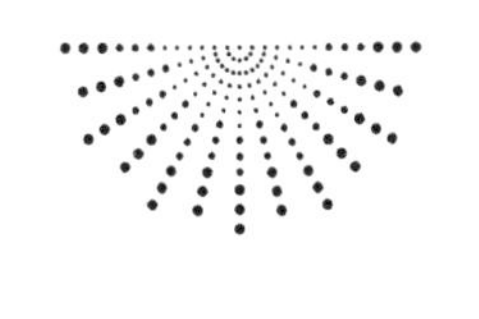

SEA SHENANIGANS

Visit robynpeterman.com for more info!

NOTE FROM THE AUTHOR

If you enjoyed reading *Petunia's Pandemonium,* please consider leaving a positive review or rating on the site where you purchased it. Reader reviews help my books continue to be valued by resellers and help new readers make decisions about reading them.

You are the reason I write these stories and I sincerely appreciate each of you!

Many thanks for your support,
~ Robyn Peterman

Want to hear about my new releases?
Visit robynpeterman.com and join my mailing list!

ROBYN'S BOOK LIST

(IN CORRECT READING ORDER)

HOT DAMNED SERIES

Fashionably Dead
Fashionably Dead Down Under
Hell on Heels
Fashionably Dead in Diapers
A Fashionably Dead Christmas
Fashionably Hotter Than Hell
Fashionably Dead and Wed
Fashionably Fanged
Fashionably Flawed
A Fashionably Dead Diary
Fashionably Forever After
Fashionably Fabulous
A Fashionable Fiasco
Fashionably Fooled
Fashionably Dead and Loving It
Fashionably Dead and Demonic

The Oh My Gawd Couple

GOOD TO THE LAST DEATH SERIES

It's a Wonderful Midlife Crisis

Whose Midlife Crisis Is It Anyway?

A Most Excellent Midlife Crisis

My Midlife Crisis, My Rules

You Light Up My Midlife Crisis

It's A Matter of Midlife and Death

The Facts of Midlife

MY SO CALLED MYSTICAL MIDLIFE SERIES

The Write Hook

You May Be Write

All the Write Moves

SHIFT HAPPENS SERIES

Ready to Were

Some Were in Time

No Were To Run

Were Me Out

Were We Belong

MAGIC AND MAYHEM SERIES

Switching Hour

Witch Glitch

A Witch in Time

Magically Delicious

A Tale of Two Witches

Three's A Charm

Switching Witches
You're Broom or Mine?
The Bad Boys of Assjacket
The Newly Witch Game

SEA SHENANIGANS SERIES
Tallulah's Temptation
Ariel's Antics
Misty's Mayhem
Petunia's Pandemonium
Jingle Me Balls

A WYLDE PARANORMAL SERIES
Beauty Loves the Beast

HANDCUFFS AND HAPPILY EVER AFTERS SERIES
How Hard Can it Be?
Size Matters
Cop a Feel

If after reading all the above you are still wanting more adventure and zany fun, read *Pirate Dave and His Randy Adventures,* the romance novel budding novelist Rena helped wicked Evangeline write in *How Hard Can It Be?*

Warning: Pirate Dave Contains Romance Satire, Spoofing, and Pirates with Two Pork Swords.

ABOUT ROBYN PETERMAN

Robyn Peterman writes because the people inside her head won't leave her alone until she gives them life on paper. Her addictions include laughing really hard with friends, shoes (the expensive kind), Target, coffee with a squirt of chocolate syrup and extra ice in a Yeti cup, bejeweled reading glasses, her kids, her super-hot hubby and collecting stray animals.

A former professional actress with Broadway, film and T.V. credits, she now lives in the South with her family and too many animals to count.

Writing gives her peace and makes her whole, plus having a job where she can work in her sweatpants works really well for her.

CPSIA information can be obtained
at www.ICGtesting.com
Printed in the USA
LVHW041850220622
721881LV00003B/377